CANNON'S REVENGE

CANNON'S REVENGE

W. W. Lee

Chivers Press   G.K. Hall & Co.
Bath, Avon, England   Thorndike, Maine USA

This Large Print edition is published by Chivers Press, England, and by G.K. Hall & Co., USA.

Published in 1996 in the U.K. by arrangement with the author.

Published in 1996 in the U.S. by arrangement with Walker Publishing Company, Inc.

U.K. Hardcover ISBN 0–7451–4740–2 (Chivers Large Print)
U.K. Softcover   ISBN 0–7451–4741–0 (Camden Large Print)
U.S. Softcover   ISBN 0–7838–1619–7 (Nightingale Collection Edition)

The text of this Large Print edition is unabridged.
Other aspects of the book may vary from the original edition.

Set in 16 pt. New Times Roman.

Printed in Great Britain on acid-free paper.

British Library Cataloguing in Publication Data available

Library of Congress Cataloging-in-Publication Data

Lee, W. W. (Wendi W.)
    Cannon's revenge / W.W. Lee.
        p.   cm.
    ISBN 0–7838–1619–7 (lg. print : lsc)
    1. Large type books.   2. Journalists—Fiction.   3. Colorado—
Fiction.   I. Title.
[PS3562.E3663C36   1996]
813'.54—dc20   95–49324

For Vera LaVerne Beatty, and in memory of Ernest T. Beatty; I couldn't have asked for better in-laws—with love.

CANNON'S REVENGE

CHAPTER ONE

Marie Dane stirred the chicken bones simmering in the large pot on the stove. Cooking over a hot stove was one of the chores she wished she could abandon during the spring and summer. Even though the Danes were doing well enough that they could have employed a woman to come in to cook and clean, Marie wasn't comfortable handing over the running of the household to a stranger. She glanced at the basket of laundry tucked away in a corner of the kitchen, then looked longingly at the blue sky through the back door. It was a beautiful day and getting out in the fresh air would be a nice change of pace.

Giving the soup one last stir, Marie wiped her hands on her apron and picked up the basket. But before she could take a step, her two-year-old daughter, Hannah, was there at her side, her rag doll hanging limply from one hand.

Marie Dane started to tell Hannah to stay inside, but changed her mind. She didn't want Hannah to be cooped up inside the house on such a bright and breezy spring day.

For the past several days Marie had had a feeling that she and Hannah were being watched while her husband was at work and the boys were in school. She hadn't actually seen anyone lurking in the woods on the edge of their property, but the feeling was there nonetheless, lying small and smoldering like the ashes of a campfire.

'All right, you can come outside with me.' Marie put the washing on the table and bent down to kiss her daughter's pale corn silk bangs. 'Just remember to stay within sight of the house, and don't go down to the creek.'

'Uh-huh,' Hannah replied, already immersed in the imaginary world inhabited by her rag doll. She hurried through the kitchen and out the back door, banging it shut behind her. Marie quickly followed.

The Danes had a good life—a grand Victorian house, a pretty little girl, and two growing boys. Just three years ago, Harold had lost his job as a printer at the *St Louis Sentinel*. They had had enough money saved to start again somewhere else and, like many others before him, Harold had had a dream of moving west and settling someplace where they could grow along with the town.

Marie had heard that the newly declared state of Colorado was welcoming settlers, so the couple packed up their sons and their belongings, moved to Deadwood, and Harold started the *Deadwood Gazette*. At first, Marie had been reluctant to settle in a town with such a dreadful name. A decade earlier, Deadwood had been a silver boomtown. When the ore was played out, the town had been saved from

2

extinction by the railroads and had become a prospering place.

Harold's newspaper was doing well, chronicling the exploits of the town's more colorful citizens and reporting on the progress of the railroad. Hannah was born the first year the family had settled in town. The Danes were looked up to by most of Deadwood as respectable citizens, and they had worked hard to gain that respect.

Of course, there had been that unpleasant situation a year ago—Marie shook her head, wanting to forget what had happened back then, the whole ugly business. She hoped that it was all behind them now. One man was dead and the other had been sent to prison, where he belonged. Stu?? Cannon had gone to see her husband after being released and had threatened him, but months had passed without incident, so Marie and Hal Dane had decided Cannon was just trying to scare them.

'Mama!'

Marie looked around, catching sight of Hannah playing by the big cottonwood near the clear stream that ran along the boundary of the Dane property. The stream was just right for washing clothes. Marie scrubbed the clothes and linens in a large metal tub that sat near the brook. Then she pulled the tub away from the tank and wrung out the wash with her strong hands. One by one, she deftly hung the dripping white bed linens out on the rope

3

strung between two thick trees in the yard. Hannah sat in the high grass by her mother's wind-whipped skirts, her doll in her lap.

'Help, Mama?'

Marie understood and chuckled. 'Yes, you can.' She showed Hannah how to wring more water out of the bottom of the hung sheets while she went back to the tub for another armful of wash. All the while, she felt uneasy. Pausing for a moment, Marie surveyed the area. The house sat on a large, open, flat lot dotted with many trees. The only concealed vantage point was a bluff that ran up the other side of the brook. She tilted her head and looked straight up the bluff, hoping that if someone were out there, he might be scared off by her directness. As she finished hanging the linens, she shook her head at the notion that anyone was watching.

She remembered the soup bones simmering on the stove and the blueberry pie she had promised Harold she would bake for tonight. 'Hannah. I'm going inside now. Are you coming?'

Hannah had been undressing her doll. She paused and shook her head, her hair shimmering in the strong sunshine.

Marie hesitated, but left the child outside.

It took only a few minutes for Marie to mix and roll out the pie dough. The early blueberries were small, and when she tested them, still sour. A little extra sugar would take

4

care of that.

When she had popped the pie in the oven, Marie looked out the kitchen window. She couldn't see Hannah. 'She's wandered off,' Marie muttered.

Quickly wiping the dough from her hands, Marie ventured out into the backyard, shading her eyes to scan the area more effectively. 'Hannah.' No response. She tried again, louder. Still no response.

Marie picked up her skirts and walked quickly to the brook, her heart beating rapidly as an unbidden thought flitted through her mind. She scanned the babbling stream, calling Hannah's name. She was met with only silence. Her breathing had become quicker and her thoughts flew wildly from one imagined accident to another.

'Hannah!' Her daughter's name echoed slightly in the wooded area around the brook. Marie bit down on her knuckle, stifling a moan. She wasn't sure what to do.

The far away sound of childish chatter made Marie Dane pull herself together. School was out and her boys, Edgar and Conrad, would be home from school soon. Edgar, nine, was the oldest. Conrad, the middle child, was two years younger.

Maybe the little girl had gone back inside, unnoticed. Marie ran into the house and searched every room thoroughly, calling Hannah's name. She wasn't there. Perhaps

Hannah had just gone up the road to meet her brothers. She had done it only a few times, each time being admonished by Marie never to do it again. Marie ran back outside.

'Ma!' Conrad yelled as he and Edgar approached the house. 'We're home.'

'Is Hannah with you?' She strained to look behind them.

Her sons slowed their pace. 'No,' Edgar said, a frown creasing his young brow. He was the more perceptive of the two boys. 'Is something wrong? Where's Hannah?'

Marie felt her heart flutter slightly. She drew a ragged breath and said as calmly as possible, 'Ed, go on back to town. Get your dad. Get Marshal Webb. Hannah's missing!'

A thin gray stream of smoke drifted out the kitchen window. No one noticed the smell of burned blueberries that filled the air.

CHAPTER TWO

Arthur Tisdale stepped off the Denver & Rio Grande train at the Deadwood station. The platform was bustling with activity, porters loading cattle and horses, ladies and gentlemen stretching their legs before going on to Denver, the stationmaster with his large railroad watch in hand, stalking the porters, making every minute count.

Finding his leather satchel among a pile of baggage in the center of the platform, Tisdale adjusted his hat and looked around.

'Arthur,' boomed a familiar, deep voice. The man who belonged to it was upon him almost immediately, pumping his hand and patting his shoulder as if to make sure Tisdale was real. Hal Dane was a medium-sized man who wore glasses that seemed too small for his features. As Tisdale had expected, Dane was dressed impeccably, even here in the small boomtown of Deadwood.

Tisdale and Dane had gotten to know each other in the cavalry and had become close friends, staying in touch even through the most difficult times. When Hal Dane had married Marie Dreyfus, Tisdale had been there to celebrate. On that day, Tisdale thought he had never seen his friend look happier. On this day, looking at his friend now, Tisdale thought he had never witnessed such sorrow in one man's eyes.

'Thank you for coming out here on such short notice,' Dane said grimly.

Tisdale gripped his friend's shoulder. 'Hal, we're friends. You knew I'd come when I received your wire. I'm so sorry to hear about Hannah. Has there been any news?'

Dane shook his head. 'We think a man named Stu Cannon might have taken her. Some of my neighbors remembered seeing Cannon ride out toward Durango. I got as far

7

as Bill Pennworth's trading post on the outskirts of Durango, and that's where I lost the trail.'

'Did Pennworth see Hannah with Cannon?' Tisdale asked.

Dane shrugged. 'Cannon didn't bring Hannah inside the trading post, but when Pennworth helped him load his supplies, he saw a small child lying asleep in the corner of the wagon on top of a bundle of clothes.'

Tisdale felt a small chill run down his spine. The two men fell uncomfortably silent, until Tisdale gently suggested, 'Maybe we'd better get back to your home, Hal.'

Dane nodded silently and led the way to his buckboard.

If it had been a visit for pleasure, Tisdale would have been impressed with the imperious house that stood at the edge of town. His friend was certainly doing quite well, but as the buckboard drew nearer to Dane's house, Tisdale stole a glance at his friend and saw the worry lines etched into the man's face, lines that hadn't been there a few years ago. Dane was only in his early thirties, but he already looked ten years older.

Tisdale had received the wire two days ago in San Francisco. All it said was: ARTHUR STOP CAN YOU COME TO DEADWOOD STOP URGENT STOP HANNAH MISSING STOP HAL DANE. Tisdale had booked himself on the next train to Denver.

Dane's wire had been too short for Tisdale to read much between the lines, but the sharp knife of fear went through his heart all the same. Tisdale had visited the Danes in St Louis, so he knew the two boys but he had never seen Hannah—even though Dane had written to him when she was born, asking his friend to act as her godparent. He remembered reading those words over and over again. He still had the letter in his possession, marking a passage in his family Bible. He had planned to give the Bible to Hannah when she became a young lady. Now there was a chance that he might never meet her, never have a chance to pass the Tisdale family Bible on to his godchild.

Just before leaving San Francisco, Tisdale had found the last letter he'd received from Jefferson Birch. Birch was working for a large cattle ranch in Kansas, just west of Cimarron, not too far from Colorado. When he got to the station, Tisdale sent a wire to Birch, letting him know that he might be needed.

During their ride out to the house, Dane said very little. Tisdale had lots of questions, but he did not press his distressed friend for details. At the house, Marie didn't come out to greet them. Instead, young Conrad slowly opened the door to let his father and Tisdale in.

'Where's your mother?' Dane asked.

Conrad shrugged wordlessly and stepped back.

'Marie,' Dane called out. Silence was the only answer. He turned to apologize. 'Excuse me, Arthur. Make yourself comfortable. I'll only be a minute.' He went down the hall toward the kitchen, then backtracked a moment later and climbed the stairs.

'We're glad you could come, Uncle Arthur,' Conrad said in a small, dull voice. 'I know Father is relieved to have you here.'

Conrad took Tisdale's valise. 'I'll just put this over by the staircase.' Tisdale took the moment alone to study the house. From the vestibule where he stood, drapery fell over every window, keeping even the smallest sliver of sunshine from entering the rooms. Candles and lanterns hung in the rooms and hallways, emitting low light, giving the house a funereal air.

'Conrad,' Tisdale returned, not sure how jovial to appear in the face of such monumental grief. 'You've grown. Soon you'll be taller than me.'

Conrad's brother stepped forward, taller, paler, with a pair of glasses perched on his nose like a sparrow balanced on a thin branch. 'Edgar,' Tisdale shook the boy's hand and gripped his shoulder with his free hand, 'you're almost a man.'

In the dim light of the entry, Dane's face seemed to appear out of nowhere. Another wan face floated into view behind him. Grief was so evident in her expression that Tisdale

10

almost didn't recognize Marie. He stepped forward and took her hands in his. 'Marie.' He fumbled for more words and found none. He felt like a stranger intruding on her grief.

'Arthur...' she whispered. Then she fell silent, pulling her hands away and looking down.

Dane cleared his throat. 'Conrad, would you please take Uncle Arthur's bag up to his room?' Without a word, the boy left. Dane turned to his other son. 'Edgar, would you please boil some water for tea?' Edgar nodded and headed for the kitchen. Dane started to go into the parlor and motioned to Tisdale to follow him. Marie stood rooted to the spot until Tisdale gently touched her elbow, then she moved mechanically into the parlor with them.

She joined her husband on the settee. Tisdale sat in the wingbacked chair across from the couple.

'Hal, tell me what happened,' Tisdale asked, leaning forward.

'Four days ago Hannah was outside playing while Marie was cooking—'

'I was only away from her a few minutes,' Marie said sorrowfully. 'I never should have let her stay out alone.'

'It's not your fault, dear. No one blames you,' Dane said to Marie, although it was clear that she blamed herself. He turned to Tisdale and continued, 'When Marie went back

11

outside, Hannah was gone. The boys came home from school and Edgar ran into town to fetch me and the marshal, while Marie and Conrad searched every inch of this place for any sign of Hannah.'

'Do you think she wandered off?' Tisdale asked, uncertain of what a two-year-old might or might not do.

'No, if she had, we would have found her,' Marie said. 'Someone took her and we both know who it was.'

Dane looked at his wife, then took a deep breath. 'I'd better start from the beginning. About a year ago, a man was gunned down outside The Big D saloon at closing time. There were several witnesses, but no one came forward right away. The man who was killed was a drifter.' Dane squeezed his eyes shut for a moment. Marie's hand lay lightly on top of her husband's. 'There wasn't a big investigation since most people already knew who the killer was—word gets around. But none of the witnesses actually came forward. The killer was the son of Stu Cannon, owner of The Big D.' Dane paused while Edgar, balancing a tea tray, came into the parlor.

Marie nodded to her son, who solemnly withdrew from the room, and she began to pour tea. Dane resumed his story. 'About a month later, a woman and two girls ride into town and it turns out that they're the wife and daughters of the dead man. Turns out the man

12

was a former bookkeeper who had gold fever. When she finds out what happened to her husband, she goes to Marshal Webb for justice, but the law's under Cannon's thumb. He tells her there's nothing that can be done. What he doesn't realize is that she's the daughter of a newspaper man and she knows the power of the press. She comes to me and asks me to remind my readers that justice must be served.' Dane shifted uncomfortably on the settee as if the memory still didn't sit right with him. 'Arthur, I can't ignore a plea like that, no matter how much pressure the marshal applies.'

'Your marshal asked you not to take up the gauntlet?' Tisdale asked.

A rueful smile appeared on Dane's face. '"Ask" is too mild a term. Webb ordered me to stay out of it, but I had no choice. This is my job. I had to write an editorial about the murder and about Mrs Anatoly's grief. My readers did the rest. Several witnesses came forward. Marshal Webb did his best to cover it up, but when it was obvious that the citizens of Deadwood were getting restless, he finally did his duty. Hugh was arrested, and there was a trial. Stu Cannon did his best to discredit the witnesses, but it wasn't good enough.'

Dane took off his glasses and pinched the bridge of his nose. 'So he turned to intimidation. He burned one man out of his house, had another man beaten up. But he was

13

caught and jailed. His son was hanged a week later. Stu Cannon got out of jail six months ago and came to my office to tell me that he would make me pay for my part in Hugh's conviction.'

'What were his exact words?'

Marie spoke up. '"I'll make sure that you suffer the way I've suffered. I've got nothing left to lose," was what he said. I was there. I'll never forget those words.'

'And now Hannah is gone?' Tisdale asked.

Dane nodded. 'I wired you the day after Hannah disappeared. There's no sign of Stu Cannon either.'

Marie described how thoroughly they had searched the house and the surrounding areas after Edgar had fetched Dane and the marshal. 'Harold insisted that the marshal call on The Big D saloon. The bartender said he hadn't seen Stu Cannon for a couple of days.'

'What about where Cannon lives? Did the marshal go there?' Tisdale asked.

Dane nodded. 'He figured that's where Cannon would be, but when he rode out there, the housekeeper told Webb that she hadn't seen him all week.'

'Did he get a posse together?'

When Marie spoke up, her tone was bitter. 'Yes. But it was the next afternoon by the time Marshal Webb organized the posse.'

Dane squeezed her hand. 'Now, Marie. You know that the townsfolk have done all

14

they can.'

A faint smile came to her tortured expression. 'Yes, they have. The Deadwood citizens have been very kind. They think it's terrible that Hannah disappeared like that, and they have been more than willing to help us. But the marshal should have done his job better. He should have rallied folks that same night and spread out to search the area. Instead, he went home to bed and didn't get a posse together until the next day.'

Tisdale cleared his throat. 'With all due respect, Marie, I know a bit about investigating and tracking people. Trying to search for a small girl in the dark is a little like trying to find your way out of a cave at nightfall. We shouldn't judge the marshal too harshly, despite his past loyalties.'

A tear rolled down Marie's left cheek and settled at the corner of her mouth. It was her only outward display of grief.

Dane stood up and paced impatiently around the parlor. 'That's why I asked you here, Arthur. I want to hire you.'

Tisdale began to protest. 'Hal, you don't need to—'

His friend cut him off. 'Please, Arthur. I know you would probably have to turn down a couple of offers of work to do this, but I couldn't trust anyone else. Besides, I've heard good things about Tisdale Investigations. You've begun to make a name for yourself.'

15

Tisdale stroked his mustache pensively. 'Hal, I won't accept payment. Hannah is my goddaughter. But I've already wired Jefferson Birch, my best investigator.'

Dane sat down again. 'I'm sure he's a good man, Arthur, but I'd feel better knowing you were handling this yourself.'

Tisdale blinked, not at all sure that his investigative powers were as strong as his friend's faith in him. 'I still will need another hand here, Hal. Birch is a great tracker.'

'Let me be your assistant. I'll do anything you say. Just tell me where to start.'

Marie put a hand on her husband's arm. 'Maybe Arthur's right, dear. He knows his business better than we do.'

Hal remained obstinate. Dane said to Tisdale, 'No matter how good this Birch is, he won't work as hard as I will to find Hannah. I'd give my life to save my baby!'

Tisdale was stymied. He knew that he needed Birch here, and hoped that his agent had gotten the wire. But Tisdale had an even more pressing problem at hand—convincing his friend to stay out of the search.

CHAPTER THREE

Jefferson Birch stuffed the wire in his shirt pocket and checked his gear one last time.

Cactus impatiently shook his mane and shifted from one leg to the other. Fred Matthews stood nearby, his left cheek bulging with chewing tobacco, dark brown spittle gathering at the corner of his mouth. 'You sure you can't stay another week, Birch? We could use you around here to help round up those strays. You got a way of finding 'em quicker than most of the greenhorns around here.'

Birch paused to look at his ranch boss. 'Thanks for the offer.' He patted his shirt pocket. 'But the news I just received can't wait another week.'

Birch had not heard from Tisdale in almost six months. The truth of the matter was that Tisdale's wire had come at the right time. He had been ready to move on, but every time he made noises about leaving, Matthews would increase his weekly pay. 'When I got a good man working for me, I try to keep him happy,' the ranch boss had said.

In fact, there was grumbling among the other cowboys because they knew that Birch was being paid far more than the average ranch worker. Birch was aware of their resentment. Even without the wire from Tisdale, Birch knew it was time for him to move on.

The wire had been short and cryptic, but Birch had a feeling that there was more to it. Tisdale had mentioned going to Deadwood, Colorado, to look for a missing child. He didn't exactly promise that there would be a

17

job waiting if Birch pushed on to Deadwood, but right now, the possibility of employment was good enough for Birch. He was flush with his pay from Matthews over the last half year, and he knew he could always get more ranch work if Tisdale decided he didn't need him after all.

The air was filled with the promise of rain as Birch left the Matthews ranch and headed west to Colorado. He figured it would take him three days of moderate riding. The trail stretched out before him, dampness closing in, and sent a chill breeze through his light cotton shirt. Birch just hoped he could get far enough tonight to find shelter from the impending storm.

*   *   *

On the third morning of Birch's journey, Deadwood lay before him like an oasis in a desert. Half of the buildings were merely tents set up to serve beer and liquor, but this was typical of a boomtown—or what had once been a boomtown. The other half of the buildings showed commitments in lumber and nails, but the majority of those looked as if there hadn't been much thought put into how they were constructed, just as long as they stayed upright.

Birch found a saloon that had thoughtfully been placed in the center of town on Main

Street. He dismounted and patted Cactus's neck before entering the place. The sign outside told him that the saloon was called The Big D.

The Big D smelled like sawdust, bear grease, and stale beer. Inside, the bartenders were kept busy with thirsty customers who rested one elbow on the bar surface and bent the other elbow whenever their glasses were refilled.

Birch was feeling parched from his long ride and ordered a beer from a whip-thin bartender with a pointed chin and pale blue eyes. He drained his beer, watching the bartenders move smoothly down the bar, refilling glasses, collecting coins, and making small talk with their regulars. Birch knew enough not to push it. Once he'd had a couple of refills, he would become a regular too.

'What's your business here, friend?' one of the bartenders asked Birch after his third beer.

'I'm trying to find the family of a missing girl,' Birch replied mildly.

The man looked up sharply, letting the beer foam over the edge of the tin mug. 'That right? What's your business with them?' he asked in a neutral tone.

Birch wanted to reply that it was none of his business, but he figured the conversation would end right then and there if he gave voice to those thoughts. 'It's not really them I need to meet,' Birch went on as if he wasn't aware of the commotion going on around him. Several regulars were listening very carefully. 'It's a friend of theirs who's come to pay a visit. Arthur Tisdale.' He paused for effect, but found no one reacting as if they had heard of Tisdale. Birch took this to mean that Tisdale and Dane had not been in town asking questions, since no one appeared familiar with Tisdale Investigations.

The bartender visibly relaxed. 'Never heard of this Tisdale, but most likely he's here on a sympathy visit.'

A man with a few days' growth and dusty clothes spoke up. 'Yeah, Dane's daughter disappeared a few days ago. He thinks Stu Cannon took her.'

The bartender gave the customer a hard look. The man stared back. 'What're you looking at, Joe? You think he won't hear it from Dane or this Tisdale fella? It's not a secret, you know.' He tossed back his whiskey and set his shot glass firmly on the bar surface. Birch set a coin down beside the glass.

'Where can I find this Dane?' Birch asked.

The bartender polished a glass nearby. The customer took up the coin. 'Thanks, friend. Hal Dane runs a newspaper, the *Deadwood Gazette*. If he isn't in his office, he lives on the east edge of town. Follow Main Street till you reach the barbershop, then take the left fork about half a mile to a big, fancy house. You can't miss it.' He turned to signal for another drink from the grim bartender.

When the drink was refilled and the bartender had moved to the other end of the bar, Birch asked, 'Why is he so angry?'

The man smiled at some private joke that he was ready to share. He sipped his whiskey this time, savoring it. 'Because Cannon, who owns The Big D, is suspected of abducting the little girl. Cannon's been missing for several days, and Joe hasn't been paid yet.'

Birch thought about that for a moment, then laid another coin next to the man's half-empty shot glass. 'Thanks for the information.'

As he started to push away from the bar, he heard the snap of a shotgun being closed. The marshal was seated in a corner of the room. He'd been cleaning his shotgun, which accounted for the smell of bear grease. A nearly empty beer bucket sat on the edge of his table, a tin mug next to it, and an empty dinner plate.

Birch was surprised that he hadn't noticed the man when he had first come in. But then, there wasn't much to notice. The marshal was a small man, round and soft-looking with rosy cheeks and a pair of gold-rimmed spectacles. His thin black hair was slicked up with the bear grease as well. But Birch's original impression changed when the man looked up—his eyes were as round and hard as pebbles of granite. Birch took an instant dislike to him, and had a feeling that he would get very little help from the marshal.

21

'My name's Webb. Marshal Darnell Webb.' Webb stood up slowly. 'I don't like strangers coming into my town and asking questions.'

'I've had all my questions answered.'

Marshal Webb narrowed his eyes. 'I hope you're not here to stir up trouble, because if you even spit in the street, I'll be there to escort you to my jail cell.'

Birch had known his share of lawmen, and for the most part, he liked the breed of man who pinned a star on his shirt and followed the law. But every once in a while, a man became a lawman for all the wrong reasons. Birch was looking at a good example right now.

Slowly, Webb cracked open the shotgun again and made a show of fishing a couple of shells off the table near him, then loading them in the shotgun. He rested the open shotgun in the crook of his arm. Despite his casual appearance, this man was sending Birch a message—and Birch was receiving it loud and clear.

'What kind of trouble would I be stirring up to go out to the Dane house?' Birch asked. He tried to appear relaxed, but he was aware of how close his right hand was to his gun.

'Questions,' was Webb's answer. 'You're asking questions about the disappearance of the little girl.'

'So what if I am?' Birch asked. 'Maybe I'm here to join in the search.'

Webb studied him for a moment, then

22

shrugged. 'The search is over. She's been gone a week. Trail's almost disappeared. It'd be better if you didn't get the Danes' hopes up.' His face darkened momentarily when he mentioned the Danes. 'Let them get on with their lives the way Stu Cannon had to get on with his life when his son was wrongfully hanged.'

'How old was the girl?'

'She was two.'

'You don't seem to be too concerned about the disappearance of a child of two from your town.'

The marshal scowled. 'Of course I'm bothered by it, but there's no evidence that Stu Cannon took her. The way I figure it, Hannah wasn't abducted like the Danes keep saying. And I think Cannon just left town because there's too many painful memories for him here.'

'Then what happened to Hannah?' Birch wanted to know.

'I think Hal Dane's wife lost track of the toddler. A cougar probably came down from the hills and carried her off.' Webb gripped the shotgun. He was an ugly man when he sneered, and Birch speculated that Webb got his position as town marshal because he knew powerful people. And he was willing to bet that one of those powerful people had been Stu Cannon. 'Now I want you out of here. I've warned you of what would happen if I catch

23

you in this town again.'

Birch left The Big D, heading in the direction his informant had given him.

CHAPTER FOUR

Stu Cannon stirred the remains of the campfire into a small flame and added another dead branch to it. He swigged down the rest of his boiled coffee and grimaced when the acid taste burned the back of his throat. A few yards away, the sleeping child was oblivious to everything that had been going on over the past few days. Cannon wasn't sure how much longer he could keep her. When they rode through Durango, he could have sworn that people looked at them in a suspicious manner. It was a good thing that he had thought to cut her hair and dress her in boys' clothes.

It had been easy to take Hannah. She had come with him willingly when he offered her barley-sugar candy. After they had traveled about half a day, she had cried, wanting her daddy and mommy, but Cannon ignored her as best he could. It disturbed him some, sacrificing this innocent child, but Hugh had been just as precious at two or three. Cannon had planned to take one of the boys, preferably the middle child, but the brothers were always together. He knew he couldn't have handled

24

both of them. He had found Hannah alone, playing outside in her yard.

At first, his plan had been to kill the child. An eye for an eye, the Bible says. But when it came down to it, he couldn't kill Hannah.

The first night, when she was fast asleep, he had stood over her, a knife in his hand, listening to the sound of her steady breathing, her small hand curled around the arm of her rag doll.

Cannon knew his son was a little wild. He'd accepted that long ago. But dammit, Hugh didn't deserve to die over some drifter. If that Anatoly woman and her brood hadn't come looking for him, nothing would have come of it. Dane hadn't cared anything about the dead man until that woman showed up and told her sob story.

Cannon felt the side of his tin mug collapsing and he loosened his grip. Anyway, it was all right now. He had figured out how to exact revenge without killing Hannah. Dane would never see his little girl again.

Cannon had determined that he just needed to find a good home for her. He figured she was young enough to forget that this had ever happened. In a few years, she wouldn't remember her old name.

When the day came that Hannah was placed in a good family, a family who knew nothing of her origins, he would leave and go someplace far away. And only then would he send a message to Hal Dane, telling him that Hannah was still alive. And that she was lost to him forever. Even if the law caught up with him, Cannon had made a vow to his dead son that he would never reveal Hannah's whereabouts.

Meanwhile, until that happened he would have to take a few precautions like he did when he changed Hannah's appearance. They'd be looking for him too. He might shave his beard while he was at it.

As the branch caught fire and flames leaped and crackled, Cannon smiled to himself, glancing at the small, still figure who slept with her thumb halfway in her mouth, her soft hair curling around her ear. He listened to Hannah take a deep breath, letting it out slowly, the grip on her rag doll tightening. One word escaped, a word mumbled in her sleep. He had heard her say it in her sleep each night for a week and he understood it well.

'Daddy.'

CHAPTER FIVE

Birch rode up into the front yard of the stately house, tethering Cactus to the fence in front and walking into the yard. Before he got halfway up to the door, a young, thin voice called out, 'Hold it, mister. What's your business here?'

Birch stopped and looked around. He couldn't see anyone, but the direction of the voice had come from around the corner of the house. 'Is this the Dane house?'

No one answered immediately, but he thought he heard a whispered conference.

'It might be,' was the vague response. 'Who are you?' The voice seemed nervous now.

'If this is Hal Dane's home, then Arthur Tisdale should be here by now,' Birch called out.

There was silence, then a rustling sound, and two pale faces popped out from behind the corner bushes. Although one boy was taller than the other by about two inches, they could have been twins. Both had suspicious looks on their faces. Both carried revolvers. The smaller boy, his hands hanging out of his pockets, took a belligerent step forward.

'Edgar, Conrad.' A woman stepped out on the front porch. Her dark hair hung limply, and she was wiping her hands on her apron. She glanced sharply at Birch before speaking. 'You'll have to forgive them, sir, they feel dutybound to protect me and themselves.'

'You must be Mrs Dane,' Birch said. 'My name is Jefferson Birch and I've traveled here from Kansas at Arthur Tisdale's request.'

Mrs Dane gave him a curious look, then stepped back toward the open front door. 'Why don't you come inside, Mr Birch. Hal and Arthur have gone to town for supplies.'

27

As Birch walked up the porch steps, he heard the two boys, Conrad and Edgar, following him from behind. Their mother arched her eyebrows and crossed her arms impatiently before addressing them. 'And you two can hand me those weapons. You know I don't approve of boys your age handling loaded guns.'

As Conrad handed his revolver over to his mother, he muttered, 'Wasn't loaded, ma'am.'

Birch detected the hint of a smile behind her stern look as she ushered her sons and Birch into the house.

'I don't know how long Hal and Arthur will be in town, Mr Birch.'

He took his hat off as he entered the vestibule. 'Too bad I didn't run into them on my way out here,' he said, crushing the brim of his hat in his hands. He wasn't usually this tense around a woman, but there was something brittle about Mrs Dane—he was afraid that she might snap at any moment.

'I could make a pot of tea while we wait, Mr Birch, or perhaps you would like something stronger?'

'Tea would be just fine, ma'am.' She withdrew to the kitchen while Birch set his hat down on an end table and strolled around the parlor, restless after his three-day ride. He could feel two pairs of eyes on his every move. Moving to the parlor doors, he peered into the dim, windowless hallway where the boys were

28

perched on the stairway.

'How do you know Uncle Arthur?' Edgar asked.

'We work together sometimes.'

Conrad shifted his legs until his back rested against the wall. Edgar's arms were tightly crossed in front of him.

'So you're here to help us find our sister?' Edgar asked.

'I guess,' Birch replied. He figured on maybe getting some information about Hannah from her brothers, if he played his cards right. 'So how old is your sister?'

Conrad spoke up. 'She just turned two. We had a party for her in May.' He turned his face toward the wall, pretending to brush some hair away from his eyes.

'What did you give her for her birthday?' Birch had never been good with children, but he knew that these boys were fiercely protective of their mother, and he wondered if they had had a chance to think about what had happened over the past few weeks.

'Ed and me helped Pa make a little wagon for her,' Conrad said. 'Ma made her a rag doll.'

'The doll's gone too,' Edgar muttered.

'We figure she still has the doll,' Conrad explained.

Birch nodded.

Another voice spoke up behind him. 'I tried to make the doll look like her.' Mrs Dane stood in the parlor door, the tray in her hands. She blinked. 'She named it Anna. We used to make jokes about Hannah and Anna.'

Birch stepped forward and gently removed the tray from her hands. With one more glance at the boys, their haunted faces watching the change in their mother's behavior, Birch led Mrs Dane to the settee. He crossed the room and closed the parlor doors, then poured the woman a strong cup of tea with several heaping teaspoons of sugar.

'Drink this,' he said, handing her the teacup.

She took the delicate cup and sipped, making a face. 'I know it's too sweet, but drink it anyway,' he urged.

When she had drained the cup, she set it down on the tray and reached into a sewing bag beside the settee. She pulled out a cheerful blue and red calico and caressed the fabric. 'I heard my boys telling you about the rag doll I made for Hannah. I made the doll dress from this material.'

'It's very nice,' he replied politely.

Mrs Dane's eyes stared into space, her expression wistful. 'I'm not very good at sewing, and that doll was the best thing I ever made. I used pale yellow yarn for the hair and blue buttons for the eyes.' She fell silent for a moment. Birch was about to ask her a question about Hannah's abduction when she added in a low, timid voice, 'I'm thinking of starting another rag doll, one that looks exactly like the one I made for her. Just for me. To remind me

30

of her. It may be all I have left, if you can't find her, Mr Birch.' She looked up at him finally, unshed tears brimming in her eyes.

This was awkward for Birch. He knew that nothing he could say would be enough to take away the pain. All he could do was hope that he found Hannah for Mrs Dane.

'I understand that Hannah has been gone for close to a week,' Birch said.

'It seems like longer,' she replied in a monotone. 'It was my fault. I left her outside. Alone.'

Birch leaned forward. 'When the boys were about the same age as Hannah, did you leave them alone outside sometimes?'

She nodded, uncertain as to where he was taking this. 'And they're still here, aren't they?' he continued.

Mrs Dane got up from the settee and walked over to the fireplace. She wrapped her arms around each other in the same manner as her son had on the staircase. 'I feel guilty all the same.'

Birch stood up as well when he heard a wagon creaking to a halt outside and horses gently nickering. The boys all but tumbled down the staircase and threw open the front door. It was the first time Birch had witnessed Edgar and Conrad act their age.

'Uncle Arthur!' Birch heard a childish voice call out. 'Did you bring us anything?'

'I believe the men are back, Mr Birch,' the

lady of the house said. 'If you'll excuse me—'
She took up the tea tray and walked back to the kitchen.

Birch strode out of the parlor to the front door. An average-looking man, purportedly Hal Dane, was unhooking the horses from the buckboard while Birch's employer, Arthur Tisdale, was surrounded by the two boys. Tisdale held a sack filled with licorice whips and hard candies. 'I don't think these can be eaten until after supper.' Tisdale looked up and blinked in surprise, and what Birch took to be relief. 'Birch! However did you—'

The tall Texan came forward. 'I got your wire and was ready to move on. So I decided to come by this way to see if you needed my services.'

The other man had stopped taking care of the horses and was standing quietly by Tisdale's side, looking Birch up and down. Birch detected a slightly suspicious look, coupled with curiosity.

Tisdale turned to him. 'Hal, this is Jefferson Birch, one of my best agents. I told you I wired him before I left San Francisco.'

'The wire was vague,' Birch explained, 'but I was heading this way and thought I'd just stop by to get the whole story.'

'And did you get the whole story, Mr Birch?' Dane asked, his eyes on his wife and boys.

Birch glanced at Mrs Dane, but she avoided his eyes. 'I just got here a few minutes ago, but some people in town gave their versions of the truth. Your boys and wife talked to me a bit, but I'd like to hear it from you.'

Dane closed his eyes. Tisdale placed his hand on his friend's shoulder and said, 'Why don't we go inside.'

It was an hour later when Birch felt he had a complete picture of what had happened and why. 'So, Mr Birch, what do you think?' Dane asked. Birch got the feeling that Dane wasn't too happy to see him, but he had no idea why.

Mrs Dane—Birch had learned that her first name was Marie—announced that supper was ready, and everyone sat down to a roast, potatoes, gravy, and biscuits. When they had polished off a dessert of peach cobbler, Dane suggested that they move into the den, where he took out his pipe, packed some shag into the bowl, and lit it.

'I appreciate your stopping by here, Mr Birch, and I thank you for your offer of help, but Arthur has already agreed to let me accompany him while he tracks down the bastard who took my daughter.' Dane's voice cracked on the last two words.

Tisdale, who was seated slightly behind Dane, threw a panicked look at Birch and shook his head. 'Hal, I would like Birch to stay on. His tracking abilities are better than mine.'

Dane turned and gave his friend a quizzical look. 'I'm sorry, Arthur. I guess I started to take over the investigation. That's your
33

territory.' He turned to Birch. 'I apologize, Mr Birch. I didn't mean to belittle your talents or turn away your offer of help. Of course, you're welcome to come with us.'

'No harm done,' Birch replied.

Tisdale gave Birch and Dane a pale smile. 'I think I'm going to step outside for a little air before turning in. We have a big day tomorrow.' He stood up. 'Will you join me, Birch? I'd like to find out what you've been doing these last few months.'

Outside, away from the house, Tisdale let out an exasperated breath.

'You seem to be having some trouble organizing this posse,' Birch observed mildly.

'Hal's a great friend, but he's so damn worried about his daughter that he's thwarting my efforts. I'm relieved that you've come. I was about to send you a second wire, but Hal has been stuck to my side all day and seems to think that I'm the only one for the job. He's got it in his head that because I operate an investigations agency, I'm the expert in tracking down kidnapped children.' By the light of the full moon, Birch thought he could see Tisdale's face flush at this admission. In the recent past, Tisdale and Birch had worked together—not a situation Birch preferred—and had more than once almost come to blows over the way an investigation was being handled. But Birch usually closed the case on his own.

'We've worked together before. We tracked down Clem Johnston,' Birch said in a kind tone, referring to a man who had been wanted for a murder he didn't commit.

Tisdale gave Birch a wry glance. 'I appreciate the vote of confidence, but you solved the case. And I only managed to get myself abducted.'

'But you also knew how to read that Paiute's signs, and that got us pointed in the right direction.' Birch hoped that Tisdale wouldn't need his self-confidence built up much longer. Although he didn't object to working with Tisdale, it would be intolerable to track Hannah and her abductor with the grieving father questioning every move.

Tisdale seemed to be thinking along the same lines. He nodded decisively. 'I've got to find a way to convince Hal that his presence is needed here more than it is out on the trail.'

Tisdale turned and went back into the house. Birch stayed outside for a while, listening to the sounds of crickets chirping and a stream rippling somewhere out in the darkness beyond the tall grass. He hoped that Tisdale could convince Dane to stay here. Birch wished that he could convince Tisdale to do the same.

CHAPTER SIX

There was only one light burning in Hal's den. As he approached the open door, Tisdale wished he felt more confident. Hal was hunched over his desk, furiously scratching at a paper with a pen, the light of the lamp glinting off his glasses.

'I was surprised to see you wearing glasses at the train station the other day, Hal.'

Dane looked up, his eyes momentarily out of focus. He reached up and self-consciously touched them. 'It got to the point where I couldn't see the type unless I held a copy of the *Gazette* at arm's length.'

Tisdale nodded. 'What are you working on?'

Dane glanced down and smiled. 'An editorial for the next edition.'

'How often do you publish the *Gazette*?'

'Every two weeks. It takes me about a week to gather news and advertisements, then another week to set the type and print it.'

'Sounds like a lot of work.'

Hal shrugged. 'Conrad and Edgar come in to help me with the type and printing. It would take me longer without them.'

Tisdale nodded and stepped farther into the room. 'What do you plan to do with the newspaper while we're investigating Hannah's disappearance?'

Hal paused briefly. 'Well, I thought the boys would take over, with Marie's help.'

'And if you can't do it without their help, how will they do it without yours?'

His friend looked down at the work he had put aside. He took off his glasses and toyed with the gold wire frame. 'I get the impression you don't want me along for the ride, Arthur.'

Tisdale stroked his mustache and frowned. 'That's not it; I'm concerned about you. I don't think you've thought things through clearly. It seems to me that Birch is the best man to investigate this case.'

Dane looked up sharply. 'But I'm her father. And you're Hannah's godfather.'

'Yes. And as Hannah's godfather, I'm telling you that Birch is the best tracker around. And the best investigator I've ever known. He's the best man for the job, not me. We would only be in Birch's way.' It took Tisdale a moment to realize that he had included himself. He added, 'Besides, your family needs you. You have two boys here who haven't smiled or laughed much since I got here yesterday. You need to live your life as normally as possible.'

Carefully avoiding Tisdale's steady gaze, Hal slowly put his glasses back on. After a long moment, he looked up, meeting his friend's eyes, and nodded. 'I'll help as much as I can, but I'll stay out of your way. And Birch's.' Then he picked up his pen. 'See you in the

37

morning.'

Tisdale muttered good night and left. Birch was still outside, leaning against one of the corral fences, his arms crossed and the brim of his hat pulled low. If Tisdale didn't know Birch better, he'd have thought his agent was asleep.

'You had a talk?' Birch asked.

Tisdale leaned against the fence next to Birch and stared up at the full moon. A cloud was moving across it, trying unsuccessfully to cover the bright, full face. 'I talked to him. I think he's unhappy with the arrangements, but I tried to make it clear to him that there's more at stake than Hannah's welfare. His whole family is affected. Even if—' Tisdale corrected himself '—when Hannah is found, the family will be changed forever.' Tisdale could feel Birch's full attention on him now. 'I think it would be best if I stayed here with the Danes and poked around, maybe find some stone that hasn't been overturned.'

Birch remained silent, but Tisdale was well aware that his agent preferred to work alone. Over the past two years and several collaborations on assignments, Tisdale had come to consider Birch a friend. Still, he always felt that Birch had created certain invisible boundaries that Tisdale could not cross. One of those barriers was the separation of their jobs.

'So I'm going out alone,' Birch stated.

Tisdale tried to detect the relief in Birch's

38

voice, but couldn't find it. 'Looks like it.'

'Where do you want me to start?'

'We'll discuss that in the morning with Hal and his wife.' Birch pushed himself off the fence post with his boot heel. He shoved his hat brim up so Tisdale could see his eyes. 'Okay, boss. I'd better get some sleep if I'm going to outfit Cactus in the morning.'

'Mr Dane and I have enough supplies to feed a small cavalry regiment,' Tisdale couldn't resist adding in a dry voice. He noted a glimmer of amusement in Birch's eyes before he turned and headed up to the house.

CHAPTER SEVEN

'Are you sure you don't want me to pack you some more biscuits?' Marie Dane was saying to Birch as her husband and Tisdale looked on. The boys had been sent to school, reluctant to go before seeing the tall Texan ride off.

'Thank you, ma'am, but no,' Birch said patiently. 'It would just weigh me down.'

She gave him a dubious look. 'I suppose you can always forage for your supper if you run out.'

Birch almost smiled until he realized she was annoyed. His welfare was a serious matter to this woman whose child's life depended on Birch being able to find her. And he took the task seriously, but he was always amused at the speculations of those who had settled in a place and didn't know much about the life of a drifter. The truth of the matter was that he always took stock of his supplies when he came to a town. And lately, he was never more than three days' ride from civilization. Sometimes Birch wondered what the future held for those who were used to living in the wilderness— with the way towns were springing up, every hundred miles or so, he speculated that in less than a century there might not be a backcountry.

'Yes, ma'am, I've done my share of foraging. I can live off the land if I have to.'

'It's true,' Tisdale added, a shade too heartily. 'I remember one time when we were lost in the desert and—' he caught Birch's eye and stopped. 'Well, perhaps I can entertain you with that story tonight at supper when Edgar and Conrad are here.'

'They'd love to hear it,' Dane said politely. He had been distant this morning. Birch understood how hard this must be, placing the life of his little girl in the hands of a stranger.

'Mrs Dane.' Birch nodded to her. 'Mr Dane.' He turned to Hal Dane and extended his hand, locking eyes with him. Dane took his hand and they shook. Dane's grip was feeble. Birch said, 'I promise to keep you informed, and I'll do my very best out there. You'll be able to do a lot of good here in Deadwood.

You know people here and can be of help to Mr Tisdale in his enquiries.' He felt Dane's grip strengthen and saw resolve fill his eyes. Turning briefly to Tisdale, he touched his hat.

*   *   *

Earlier that morning, Hal Dane had come down to breakfast in a black mood. Tisdale had tried to talk to him, but Dane had ignored both his friend and Birch, concentrating on the burned eggs and well-done biscuits made by his wife.

'Marie, how difficult can it be to fry a couple of eggs?' He went on in this vein until his wife got up from the table and stalked silently out of the room. Birch noticed that Edgar and Conrad had eaten every scrap and sat there sullenly. It was clear to him that they were confused by this exchange. It was probably not the sort of thing they were used to hearing from their parents.

Marie Dane came back into the dining room five minutes later and, ignoring her husband, beckoned to the boys with a lunch pail in each hand.

When the boys were gone, Tisdale turned to his friend. 'Hal, I thought we discussed this last night. Birch needs as much information as you can provide him with. If you're going to be uncooperative, maybe we should both leave.'

'Don't do that, Arthur,' Marie Dane said.

41

She was standing in the doorway of the dining room, a photograph in her hand. 'This is a recent likeness of Hannah. A visiting photographer took it for her last birthday.' Birch took the photograph and studied it. She was a serious-looking little girl, standing there with hands at her sides, a thoughtful expression, almost a frown, on her features. Wispy fair hair curled around her face, and a bow had been added. She wore a white linen dress, trimmed in lace, and her best stockings and shoes. She was very pretty, a babyish version of her mother, with her father's stubborn chin and resolute eyes.

'She looks like you,' Birch said, handing the picture back to Mrs Dane.

Marie Dane smiled and refused the photo. 'You'll need it when you go on your enquiries. Just bring it back.' He thought he saw panic in her eyes, but if so, she was fighting it. She seemed much more collected than she had been yesterday.

Dane, on the other hand, was brooding and unresponsive to Tisdale's questions. He glowered at Marie as if she were betraying him instead of helping to find Hannah.

'What does Cannon look like?' Birch asked.

Dane got up from the table and left the room for a minute. When he returned, Birch was surprised to be handed a photograph of two men standing outside The Big D saloon.

Birch studied the photograph. One man,

42

who was bearded, stood outside the door, his thumbs hooked inside his suspenders. A walrus mustache covered his upper lip and mouth, a porkpie hat was perched on his large head. Gauging the height of the doorway in the picture with Birch's own visit to the saloon the day before, Cannon didn't appear to be very tall—maybe about Tisdale's height. Stu Cannon didn't look anything at all like the picture Birch already had in his mind.

Dane pointed to Cannon's beard. 'I was told by those who were there that ever since a man cut him in a fight about ten years ago, Cannon's worn that beard to hide the scar.'

'He may have shaved it off to change his look,' Birch replied.

'At least the visible scar will make it easier for us to identify him,' Tisdale added.

A dour-looking man, a younger version of Cannon, stood next to Cannon in the photograph.

'That's Hugh, his son,' Dane replied to the unanswered question. 'This was taken right before he killed Anatoly.'

*   *   *

When Birch had ridden about ten minutes, he glanced back and saw with relief that the Victorian house was no more than a spot on the horizon. He felt the weight of the family's smoldering grief lift from his shoulders and he

43

had no doubt that he would now be able to concentrate on the case. He just hoped that whatever Cannon's plan was, it didn't include killing an innocent two-year-old child.

With the end of the cold season and the advent of spring, the Colorado landscape had taken on an assortment of colors. Wildflowers grew alongside the trail: bright, fiery oranges and reds, royal purples and blues, delicate pinks and yellows seemed to mock Birch as he headed toward Durango. He wanted to talk to Bill Pennworth, the trading post owner who was the last to remember seeing Hannah and Cannon. Perhaps there was something Pennworth had caught but had dismissed as insignificant.

Dane had told Birch that Pennworth's place was right on the road to Durango. He admitted that the posse hadn't gone much farther than that, only because Durango was far enough away to discourage all but Dane. And Dane had admitted to feeling discouraged as he rode into Durango. 'I had no idea where to start. I asked questions of strangers on the street, but no one could help me or seemed willing to try.' The pain of this recollection was evident in Dane's eyes as he recounted this.

Pennworth's house, according to Dane, was located right along the trail, set back about two hundred yards. It was really still more of a shack, and Pennworth, who owned a trading post, worked on it bit by bit whenever he had

44

free time.

The shadows had almost disappeared when Birch finally came across the house. It was plain and solid on one side, but the other side looked like it had been cobbled together with whatever had been handy. The windows, which didn't appear to have glass in them, were shuttered and the door was firmly locked, making it obvious that Pennworth wasn't there. Birch reasoned that Pennworth was at his trading post, which he had been told was half a mile farther downriver.

It was a small log lodge, dark inside, the smell of bear grease, whiskey, and tobacco strong in the musty air. Pennworth was a bear of a man himself, large, with long matted hair, bushy eyebrows, and an unkempt beard. Birch wasn't certain, but some of the smell seemed to be emanating from Pennworth. He looked as if he didn't wash very often. His clothes seemed as if they could move of their own accord, if Pennworth was of a mind to take them off someday.

Birch walked up to the table where Pennworth stood. 'Bill Pennworth?'

The big man was bent over a hide, inspecting it for flaws. He looked up at Birch, but stayed bent over the skin.

'I understand you saw Stu Cannon a few days ago.'

Pennworth straightened up, frowning. 'Cannon. The name sounds familiar.' His faint

45

British accent surprised Birch.

'The man who abducted a little girl from her home in Deadwood, about thirty miles from here.'

Pennworth nodded. 'Oh, yes. I remember Mr Dane coming here to talk to me a few days ago.' He shook his head slowly. 'Terrible thing, that. But I'm not sure how much more help I can be.'

'I just wanted to hear the story from you. I was heading to Durango anyway and thought I'd stop by.'

Pennworth came out from behind the table and gestured for Birch to follow him. 'It's been slow today. I don't expect anyone to come by, so why don't we retire to the back of the store and have a drink.'

The back room was much like the front room, only it was smaller and more crowded with hides and tobacco. 'I keep the good stuff here.' Pennworth pulled a box out of a corner and rummaged through it, producing a small canister of tea.

'Black tea from China,' he said, beaming as he put a blackened kettle on the woodstove that sat against one wall. 'It's a habit I haven't been able to lose. I am the youngest son of a duke, the black sheep of the family.' While he prepared a chipped porcelain teapot for the loose tea, he talked about the afternoon he had seen Stu Cannon.

'I saw a wagon pull up near the fence. A man

46

got out. He had a water skin in his hand. He asked for water and bought some supplies.'

'Did you see a little girl?'

Pennworth nodded. 'Just for a second, when I helped him load up. She was sleeping in the back of the wagon.' He stroked his beard. The kettle was boiling and he poured water over the tea leaves, then let it sit for a minute. 'You think you can find this man?'

'I hope so.' Birch was beginning to see just what a big job this was going to be. 'Did he say anything else, maybe give you an idea of where he was headed?'

'He didn't talk much. But after he thanked me, they headed in the direction of Durango.' He poured the thick black liquid into the mugs he had gotten out earlier. 'Would you like lemon or cream? I just acquired a small box of lemons from a man traveling north.' Birch took his tea black. Tea was an unusual commodity here in the West and he didn't have it very often. Of course, if he had a choice, he would have preferred whiskey. As if reading his mind, Pennworth produced a flask. 'You look like more of a bourbon man.' Birch smiled and held out his mug.

The bourbon cut the bitter taste of the tea. They sat in silence for a few minutes, sipping their tea and bourbon, before Pennworth asked, 'What do you plan to do from here?'

'Go on to Durango. Ask questions. Find someone who remembers them.'

'A man traveling with a little girl is a mite unusual.'

Birch shrugged. 'Most people would just assume that the mother had died or that it's just a man taking his little girl into town for the day. I have to hope that Cannon did something out of the ordinary, something that would make a person think it a bit strange.'

Pennworth tossed back the dregs of his tea. 'I don't envy you. It's a tall order.' He brightened momentarily. 'I just remembered something.' Birch leaned forward. 'He asked me if I had a pair of scissors. I'd just sold my last pair the day before.' He paused, then said, 'I don't suppose that helps you much, does it?'

Birch nodded thoughtfully. 'It may not seem like much, but I have to wonder why he would want a pair of scissors.'

Pennworth went outside with Birch to see him off. 'It's about two hours to Durango if you stick to the trail.'

'Thanks for your help.' Birch swung up on the saddle. 'And for the tea.' He suppressed a smile. Sometimes people could surprise him. Pennworth appeared to be a rough man, someone most men would think twice about talking to, but by the end of their conversation, Birch had begun to see gentility beneath the rough exterior. He hoped that whatever Pennworth had been looking for, he had found.

CHAPTER EIGHT

Durango was a big town, legendary for the gunslingers who passed through and shot up the saloons in the lawless days of the West. Now that Marshal Walker had arrested or run the outlaws out of town, it was a fairly quiet place to live and work. Horse ranches surrounded the edges of Durango, which was becoming known as the place to go for a good string of working horses. Stables had sprung up in the center of town, and buyers and sellers haggled over prices while the railroad waited to ship the horses to the east coast or south to Texas and New Mexico.

Birch rode on the edge of the main street, keeping a watchful eye out for speeding wagons. At the first general store, he stopped and tethered Cactus to the hitching post. If Cannon had been interested in a pair of scissors, he would probably stop at the first store he came to in Durango.

Inside, the smell of pickle brine was strong. The top of the pickle barrel was leaning against a post and a muscular man was bent over the barrel, fishing for the largest pickle he could find. Glass jars filled with sweets were lined up behind the counter, and bolts of brightly colored cloth were stored above the candy. A line of shiny scissors hung from hooks beneath the fabric. An attractive woman in her early thirties stood behind the counter like a regiment sergeant, keeping a watchful eye on the customer.

'I swear, Calvin, if you were given a nickel, you'd be wondering why it wasn't a dime,' she said to him. 'Will you just grab a pickle and get your grimy hands out of my barrel? Pretty soon, I won't be able to tell the difference between the pickles and your fingers.'

Calvin stood up, a fat green pickle between his fingers, a look of triumph on his face. 'Mother always taught me to get the most value for my money.' He tossed a nickel to her and she caught it deftly, as if they went through this ritual every day. Biting into his prize with a satisfying crunch, Calvin strolled out of the store. 'See you tomorrow, Emily.'

Emily shook her head in mock disgust. It was clear to Birch that she enjoyed her exchange with Calvin.

Birch approached the counter, catching sight of a small wooden sign hung on the wall that said MISS EMILY WANAMAKER, PROPRIETOR.

'Miss Wanamaker?'

She turned her face to him and smiled. 'May I help you, sir? Let me guess.' She eyed him, her eyes eventually stopping at his holster. 'You look like you could use a box of bullets for that Navy Colt. I just hope you're not a gunfighter.'

Birch cocked his head. 'Why?'

She smiled. 'Our marshal doesn't like troublemakers. He lumps all men who wear their guns low in the same category.'

'I might just have come in here for a new saddle blanket.' Birch was enjoying the banter, but he was aware that behind her light conversation, she was warning him to be careful. 'Besides, I'm not a gunfighter.'

She cocked her head to the side. 'Bounty hunter?'

Birch adjusted the brim of his hat. 'Sort of. I'm on a job, trying to track a man who abducted a little girl.'

Miss Wanamaker's smiling face suddenly turned serious. 'Oh, my. There was a man who came in here about a week ago, asking me the same question. I'm afraid that I can't help you. I haven't seen any men accompanied by a little girl lately. At least, none that I didn't already know. Mike Burnside comes in here with his ten-year-old, Rosalie. But that's because his wife died this past winter.'

Birch's heart sank. He was going over the same ground as Hal Dane. He had been arrogant enough to assume that Dane didn't know what he was doing. 'There's some new information. Maybe he didn't come in here with her—he might have come in alone to buy a pair of scissors.' He looked up at the row of bright blades for emphasis.

Miss Wanamaker frowned in recollection. 'Most of my scissors customers are women, but yes, I recall a man coming in here and buying a pair of scissors. He was scruffy looking and didn't have a child accompanying him.'

It wasn't much, but Birch felt elated, as if he had taken one minute step toward finding Hannah. 'Did he mention what he would be using the scissors for?'

She shook her head. 'No, and I'm afraid I didn't ask. I assumed that he was buying them for a wife or mother, or maybe using them himself. Some miners and wilderness men have come in here to buy scissors because they repair their own clothes, but not lately. Except for the man I just mentioned.' She brightened. 'Oh, yes. I just remembered something. He bought boys' clothes. A pair of denims and a cotton shirt.'

'What size?'

She thought for a moment. 'Small enough for a two- or three-year-old to wear.'

Birch leaned forward. 'Did you have the door to the store open that day? Maybe you saw the horse he was riding.'

She closed her eyes for a moment, then opened them and shook her head, clearly disappointed. 'We had fairly miserable weather last week, rainy and cold. But I believe he came in here around this time of day.'

'Would your customer, Calvin, have seen him?'

Her eyes lit up. 'I believe he might have. Calvin comes in here the same time every day.

52

Go talk to him. He might have seen something. He has a smithy shop down the street, The Black Horse.'

Birch thanked her and left. The Black Horse emanated the odor of fire and brimstone. Birch had never enjoyed going to the blacksmith, and Cactus acted a little nervous, side-stepping outside the place as if he were due for a shoeing.

The double doors were open to let out some of the heat, and Calvin was seated at an anvil, hammering away at a red-hot iron shoe when Birch entered. When he had finished hammering, Calvin inspected the shoe and, satisfied with its symmetry, plunged it into the nearby bucket of water, making the hot metal hiss and steam.

'You look familiar,' Calvin said by way of a greeting. 'Where have I seen you before?'

'Miss Wanamaker's General Supply.'

The smithy nodded. 'Your horse throw a shoe? I can have one ready for you within an hour.'

'No, but thanks. I'm looking for information. Miss Wanamaker thought you might be able to help.'

The mention of Emily Wanamaker brought a smile to the blacksmith's grimy face. 'I'll do whatever I can. What do you need to know?'

Birch explained the abduction and the man who had bought scissors and boys' clothes in the general store. Calvin nodded thoughtfully. 'I recall something like that. It was raining and

53

I remember thinking I should have worn a coat. As I entered the store, he was on his way out. He brushed past me and got into a buckboard. There was an oil tarpaulin over the open wagon, so there could have been a child hidden under there.' He had unconsciously grabbed an iron bar with both hands and the muscles strained as he tried to bend it. Birch swore he saw the bar buckle slightly in the middle. Calvin came back to the present and looked down at the bar. 'Sorry. I was thinking about what that man did to that family and to that little girl. I hope you get him, stranger, because if he crosses my path before you catch up with him, there won't be enough left of him to use to grease a gun.'

'I appreciate your help.' Birch touched his hat and turned to leave, then thought better of it. 'If you do hear anything else from other people here in town who might remember him, or the girl, please send a wire to this man.' Birch took Tisdale's wire out of his pocket and, using a pencil from his pocket, scratched Dane's name and the town of Deadwood on it and handed it to Calvin.

Calvin took the paper and tucked it carefully into an accounting book that had been placed away from the fire. 'You might want to try asking around some of the restaurants on the way out of town, on the road to Yellow Jacket. He might have stopped there for something to eat. Maybe one of the restaurant proprietors remembers serving a man and girl.'

'Thanks. I'll try that.' Birch tipped his hat and left.

Birch tried several restaurants without results until he passed the Dixie Restaurant. It was a spotless place with five tables and a long counter toward the back. The place was empty. A copper urn behind the counter let out steam and the thick scent of coffee.

A young woman came out of the kitchen, followed by a rich, meaty aroma that made Birch's stomach rumble. 'You can sit anywhere. I've just made a pot of buffalo stew. Would you like some?'

Birch nodded, took his hat off, and sat at the counter. 'Coffee, too.'

She poured coffee from the urn into a thick, white mug and set it in front of Birch. She stepped back into the kitchen and came out a moment later with a large bowl of stew in one hand and a plate of fried bread in the other. Birch dug into the stew, realizing how hungry he was. The young woman slowly wiped down the copper urn. 'You passing through?' she asked.

'Yes. I'm looking for a man and a little girl.'

She frowned. 'Friends of yours?'

For the fourth time that day, Birch launched into his story. As he neared the end, the urn was spotless from vigorous polishing. The woman turned around, angry tears in her eyes.

She tossed the rag on the counter and wiped

55

her hands on her apron. 'How can I help?'

'They passed through Durango a few days ago, and there's a slim chance that they stopped here for a meal,' Birch explained, taking out the photograph of Hannah and showing it to her. She studied it for a long time, then shook her head. 'I haven't seen her.' She looked up at Birch, regret in her eyes. 'I wish I had.'

Birch thanked her, paid his bill, and turned to leave. 'Wait,' she said. 'One day last week, I had to wait at the train station for supplies, and my mother did the cooking. It took me almost all afternoon to supervise the unloading of the crates and to check and double-check the inventory.'

Birch waited, wondering whether to get his hopes up. She seemed to sense this and smiled. 'Wait here. I'll go fetch my mother. We live above the restaurant.'

A few minutes later, the young woman came back, accompanied by an older version of herself. She was blushing slightly. 'I'm sorry. I forgot to introduce myself. Delores Owen.'

Her mother patted Delores's shoulder. 'She forgets her manners sometimes. I'm Helen Thomas.' Birch noted the difference in last names.

Birch introduced himself. 'Your last name is different from your daughter's.'

Helen sobered briefly. 'Delores lost her husband last year. That's why I came out west, to help my daughter start this restaurant.'

'I'm sorry.' Birch looked around at the neat little place again. 'You certainly make a good stew.' He changed the subject, giving Mrs Thomas a brief account of what he was looking for and why. He showed her the photograph.

She nodded in thought, studying it before handing it back to him. 'I don't recall a man and a little girl. For the noontime meal, we mostly get people who work nearby. Usually, families come in for dinnertime.' She fell silent again, thinking. Finally, she said, 'There was a man who came in here at noon. He had a little boy with him, not a little girl. I'm sorry I couldn't have been more help.'

Birch thought about the scissors and the boys' clothes. He held the photograph out to her again. 'Try to remember what the boy looked like. Was he about this age? Could it have been a girl in boys' clothes?'

Mrs Thomas gave him a dubious look before glancing at the photograph again. After a minute, she nodded. 'It could be the same one. The boy seemed pretty unhappy.'

'Did the man and boy do or say anything unusual?'

'No, but the boy never once called the man Pa. I assumed that the man was an uncle or family friend.'

'Where does the road lead from here?'

Delores answered. 'To Yellow Jacket. It's about a hundred miles from here.'

Birch nodded to both ladies. 'Thank you. You've both been very helpful.'

'Mr Birch?' Delores Owen's hands were clasped together. She looked very young and vulnerable in the afternoon sun. 'If you find her, will you please let us know?'

'You can be sure of that, Mrs Owen.' Birch smiled and left.

CHAPTER NINE

Tisdale entered Dane's office. 'We received a wire from Birch.'

Dane looked up from the printer's tray, his ink-stained hands picking out letter blocks that were scattered across the worktable. He pushed a lock of hair out of his eyes. 'What does he say? Has he found a clue?' He reached forward eagerly for the slip of paper and read it. His face fell. 'All it says is that he's going on to Yellow Jacket. He's picked up a possible lead.'

'Now, Hal. You don't know Birch like I do. If he's following a trail, he has good reason to do so.'

Dane looked up. 'We should go there, Arthur.'

'Go where?' a bewildered Tisdale asked.

'To Durango. Yellow Jacket. We should go see for ourselves what your agent found out.

58

Maybe I could be of some help.' Dane started to wipe his hands on a nearby rag. 'We could leave right now and be in Durango by sundown.'

'No, Hal. Let Birch handle it.' Tisdale said this firmly. 'It's not the right time.'

'Arthur, I've gone along with this plan up until now, but—when *is* the right time?'

Tisdale smiled grimly. 'We won't have to ask, Hal. We'll just know.'

The door opened and a man stepped inside, hat in hand. He looked around, seemingly unsure of his surroundings. He wore a dusty jacket and was in need of a shave. In his hand, he held a copy of the *Deadwood Gazette*. Dane walked to the front. 'May I help you?'

The man nodded. 'I'm not sure. It may be more like I'm helping you, or whoever ran this article on the missing little girl.'

Tisdale came forward, slightly suspicious of this man. Dane had written an article for the last issue of the *Gazette*. It would appear in every paper until Hannah was found, even if it took the rest of his life. The article included an offer of a reward for information leading to Hannah. Tisdale had been against the reward because it attracted unscrupulous types.

'You have information on my daughter?' Dane leaned forward eagerly.

'M-maybe,' the stranger stuttered, eyeing Tisdale uncertainly.

'What kind of information?' Tisdale asked

59

sternly, narrowing his eyes.

The man shifted from one foot to the other, his eyes traveling down to the floor. 'I understand there's a reward, but you don't say how much.'

'Oh, so you'll only give us the information for a price,' Tisdale said, jumping in before his friend could offer the money. 'How do we know that the information is any good?'

'Arthur,' Dane said quietly.

'Oh, no,' the man replied, shaken by Tisdale's accusation. 'It's just that, well, I haven't eaten since yesterday, and I lost everything I own in a stake that was played out. I just thought since I think I may have seen them—'

'You saw them?' Dane reached forward and grabbed the man's shoulders, startling him.

'Y-yes, I think so.'

'Where?'

'Redmesa. I think I saw them in Redmesa. It was a man like in your description here, and a little girl.' The man was shaking now.

'How long ago?' Dane asked.

'About two days ago.'

Dane reached into his pocket and withdrew some money, cramming it into the stranger's hand. 'Thank you, sir. You've given us hope.'

The man left, nervously backing out the door. 'Thank you. Thank you very much. I hope you find your daughter.'

Dane spun around to face Tisdale. 'We've

got to wire Birch, tell him he's on the wrong trail. He has to go to Redmesa.'

'How far is Redmesa from Yellow Jacket?' Tisdale asked.

'About fifty miles. Actually, Redmesa's closer to Deadwood. We're only half the distance from it because we're farther south.' Dane began pacing.

'Hal—'

'Maybe we can go there instead,' Dane continued as if he hadn't heard Tisdale, 'let Birch continue what he's doing in Yellow Jacket.'

'Hal—'

'You said yourself that if he's headed that way, he has good reason—'

Tisdale raised his voice slightly this time. 'Hal.'

Dane looked up as if he was surprised that Tisdale was still there.

'I'll go. Alone.'

'Arthur, this is my little girl.'

'And Marie's. Are you going to bring her along on what may possibly turn out to be a wild goose chase? What about the boys? Should they go along as well? And what about your paper? I know you think everyone can get along without you for a while, but the truth of the matter is that you're needed right here in Deadwood, bringing that paper out every week. How do you think you got that man to come in here in the first place?'

61

Dane stared at his friend for a full minute before dropping his head in defeat. 'You're right. You go. Someone has to stay here in case Hannah is found or information comes in through my editorials in the *Gazette*.'

Tisdale clapped his friend on the shoulder. 'If it turns out to be a promising lead, we'll bring Birch in. He can handle a man like Cannon.'

'Why don't you go back to the house and tell my wife,' Dane replied, his shoulders slumping slightly. He rubbed his eyes. 'She can get you the supplies you need for your trip.'

Tisdale ignored the tear that slid down his friend's face.

CHAPTER TEN

A light spring rain had begun just outside Durango and had become a full-blown cloudburst by the time Birch got as far as Hesperus. He hadn't realized that there was a town between Durango and Yellow Jacket. No one had mentioned it. But then, the town wasn't much to talk about. It consisted of one way station converted into a trading post, a tent that served as room and board for passing travelers, and a stable. There were a few other shacks scattered around, but it barely qualified as a town.

A man came out of the room and board tent, his face still raw from a fresh shave, and tossed the contents of a bowl of soapy water onto the dirt trail that ran past the shelter. Birch reined in Cactus.

'You lost, stranger?' the man asked. He was short and round, his red long johns bleached almost pink from numerous washings. A pink scalp showed through his strands of pure white hair.

Birch dismounted from his horse and looked around. 'Is this all there is to Hesperus?'

'Yep.' The man tossed the bowl back inside the tent and rubbed his jaw as if it ached.

'How far to Yellow Jacket?'

'A long day by horse.'

Birch looked around, wondering how else anyone would get there. He supposed some people might want to leave Hesperus bad enough to go by foot. 'Do many travelers come through here?'

The man scratched his armpit. 'A few. I haven't seen anyone come through in a few days.'

Birch showed Hannah's photo to the man, who shook his head and said, 'Dressed as a boy, you say? Hard to tell from this here picture. I seen a young boy just the other day, traveling with a man. I thought they were father and son. They were headed toward Yellow Jacket, all right.' He handed the photo back to Birch, then spat in the dirt. 'You know, you may run into Doc Henry in Yellow Jacket. You should talk to him. He left with the man and boy, although they probably traveled faster than Doc and eventually parted ways. Doc travels around these parts, dispensing his bottled Indian medicine, a dime a bottle. Just plain watered whiskey, if you ask me. But he makes a living, and folks around these parts are happy to buy it, and even happier after they start drinking it.'

Birch had always been skeptical of medicine shows, and even more skeptical of the men who sold those bottles. But he was willing to put his prejudice aside if Doc Henry knew something about Hannah and Cannon. Hell, Birch would buy up all the medicine bottles the wagon carried if this Doc Henry knew something that would lead to recovering Hannah.

He rode straight through Hesperus and kept going toward Yellow Jacket. It was midafternoon when he came across a colorful wagon parked by the side of the trail near a small stream. A slender young Indian woman in a calico dress was bent by the water, scrubbing clothes on a flat rock. Several pairs of wet long johns hung on the branches that bent over the brook.

An older man with a white walrus mustache, a white brimmed hat, and red suspenders was tending to the two horses when Birch rode up.

The man looked up. 'Howdy.'

Birch slid off Cactus. 'I'd like to rest here for

a few minutes, if that's all right with you. My horse needs water.'

The man detached himself from the two horses. 'Sure it is. Glad for the company. My name's Doc Henry.'

Birch nodded to the side of the wagon, which proclaimed in large, ornate gold letters, DOC HENRY'S INDIAN MEDICINES—GOOD FOR WHAT AILS YOU. 'I figured,' Birch said before introducing himself and explaining his mission.

Doc Henry listened intently, nodding occasionally, stroking his magnificent white mustache thoughtfully. 'I remember 'em from Hesperus. The boy, er, girl, had a cough and the man bought a bottle of my medicine. He seemed real concerned. I didn't think it was anything to worry about.'

Birch showed Hannah's photograph to Doc. 'It looks like it could be the boy I saw. Around the same age, fair hair.' Doc Henry said this hesitantly, then shook his head sorrowfully. 'Problem is, could be a picture of almost any child.'

Birch understood.

Doc called his assistant over. 'Mary!' He caught Birch's raised eyebrows. 'It's her Christian name. Most people couldn't pronounce her Indian name. But then, she still can't speak a word of English.'

The young woman came over. She was beautiful in an exotic way, her long black hair braided down her back, her high cheekbones and dark, flashing eyes under proud arched brows.

Doc Henry spoke to her in halting Crow. She listened quietly, unmoving. When he was done, he gestured for Birch to show her the photograph. Mary studied it without touching it. She murmured something to Doc Henry, who said, 'I'm sorry, Mr Birch. She told me that all white children look alike to her. She couldn't be certain this is the same child as the one we saw.'

Birch thanked them. It occurred to him that if Doc Henry and his medicine wagon had left Hesperus yesterday, they should be farther along the road.

'If you don't mind my asking, why are you here? If you left Hesperus yesterday, you should be in Yellow Jacket by now.'

Doc pulled a handkerchief out of his pocket and wiped his forehead. 'If you look on the other side of the wagon, you'll see why.'

Birch went around to the other side and saw the problem—the front wagon wheel had gotten stuck in a rut. 'Your horses can't pull it out?' He glanced at the two animals and realized that one of them was a little long in the tooth.

'I've tried, they've tried, Mary's tried. We can't get it out of this rut and I'm afraid of breaking an axle if it doesn't ease out of there on its own.'

Birch went down and studied it. The ground had hardened around the bottom of the wheel, and when he tried to break it, it was almost as hard as stone. 'Clay,' he said. 'Let's build a fire and warm up some creek water. We'll soak it until the clay can be removed and the wheel can move without breaking.'

It took several hours, but eventually the horses were hooked up to the wagon, Cactus in the lead, and the wagon was eased out of the rut undamaged. Mary had become more comfortable in Birch's presence, perhaps even grateful for his help in getting the wagon back on the trail. While Birch told Doc about Cannon, Mary cooked a meal for the three of them.

'How far are we from Yellow Jacket?' Birch asked. He was anxious to get back on the road. He needed to check the telegraph office for messages from Tisdale, although he didn't hold out much hope.

'Not far,' Doc replied. 'Maybe half a day. I think we'll get started in the morning. You're welcome to stay around our wagon.'

Birch looked at the setting sun. A chill was in the air, and the crickets had begun to chirp, another sign of nightfall. He could go on without the medicine wagon, but it was getting dark and Yellow Jacket was far enough away for Birch to decide to bed down with Doc and Mary for the night. He pulled his saddle off Cactus and brushed his horse down, then got his bedroll out and settled down for the night.

CHAPTER ELEVEN

A group of adobe buildings on a low plateau, Redmesa rose up before Tisdale. The farther south he had ridden, the hotter it had become. The wind caused the red dust to blow across the trail and comb the yellow grass like invisible fingers through long blond hair.

The town looked like a ghost town from where Tisdale sat, but he had heard from Hal Dane that Redmesa was a small community of Ute, Arapaho, and Cheyenne Indians who had been removed from their lands to make room for the gold boom that had brought so many easterners out west. Colorado had been struck with gold fever in the sixties, and it hadn't abated.

Tisdale shifted uncomfortably in his saddle, and idly wondered how Birch could make his living on a horse. He longed for his office in San Francisco, his desk and the squeaky swivel chair with the rollers that let him push off and travel across the room in a matter of seconds. Instead, he had been sitting atop a swaybacked mare for seven hours, and he longed to walk around on firm ground again.

Several saloons and general stores dotted the placid town. The main thoroughfare was silent as he rode down it, but a few Indians squatted in the shade of the covered walkways. Tisdale finally dismounted outside the law office. Along with the many Indians who lived in Redmesa, there were a number of white men as well. Situated between Yellow Jacket and Sunrise, Redmesa was officially recognized as a town, and as such, was in need of law and order.

The marshal's office was cool inside, a patchwork of sunlight and darkness laying across the packed dirt floor. A short, thin man with whiskers came into the room through a back door.

Tisdale took off his hat and nodded. 'Are you the marshal?'

The man put one hand on his gunbelt. 'Who wants to know?'

Tisdale introduced himself. 'I'm on the trail of a man named Stu Cannon. He abducted a little girl, and I'm looking to get her back to her family.' He went on to explain the situation, describing Cannon the way Dane had described him.

When Tisdale finished, the lawman nodded his understanding. 'I don't recall seeing 'em, but then, I been away from here for about a week. Let's see what we can do. I'll take you around to meet the people who might have seen them.' Tisdale followed the marshal out the door.

It was two hours later when they came across

the boy who watched the stables. He recognized the description of Cannon. 'Yeah, a powerful-looking feller. Mean face and a scar on his neck. I remember him. Still here, but might leave town tomorrow morning.' Tisdale held his breath. It seemed too good to be true. The stable boy continued, 'But he don't have no little girl with him.' It had been too good to be true.

'Was there anyone with him?' Tisdale asked.

'Nope,' the boy replied. 'He's alone. Said he was driftin', lookin' for work. He's staying at Miz Rhodes's boardinghouse, near your office, Marshal.'

'Damn,' the marshal said. 'Let's go arrest the bastard.'

'No,' Tisdale said, thinking quickly. 'If the girl's not with him, I don't want to scare him into not talking. Maybe he has her hidden somewhere. I think I'd better just follow him. Please don't let on that anyone's trailing him.' He looked at the marshal and the boy, who both agreed to keep silent. 'Now, where's your telegraph office?'

The marshal gave him directions. Tisdale thanked him. He wasn't sure how to proceed from here, but he knew that he would have to send a wire to Birch.

Tisdale had just left the Redmesa telegraph office when he saw a man who fit Cannon's description come out of a restaurant across the street. He followed the big man down the street

70

to a small house near the marshal's office. A sign on a post announced room and board. As Tisdale casually walked past, he noticed a buckboard by the side of the house. He had been told that Cannon's buckboard had faded red sides, and from what he could see, the buckboard next to the house had faded red sides.

Excitement shot through Tisdale. He went up to the house. A pleasant-faced middle-aged woman answered his knock. 'Are you looking for a bed for the night?' she asked as she looked him up and down. He apparently passed her inspection because she turned her smile up a notch.

'Yes, I was just passing through town, but I'm tired of the trail. I'd like a bed for the night and a home-cooked meal.'

'You've come to the right place,' the woman said, stepping inside and gesturing for Tisdale to do the same.

The front parlor was cheerful, with a blue damask settee and matching chairs, ivory wallpaper, and mahogany furniture. The woman said her name was Margaret Rhodes. 'I started this boardinghouse three years ago after my husband died. What do you do, Mr Tisdale?'

Tisdale had already thought of a cover. 'I'm in land speculation.'

'Oh, a gold miner,' she replied.

'Actually, I'm acquiring stakes for buyers

71

back east,' he replied. He was wondering how smart it was to rent a room in the same boardinghouse as the man he had under surveillance.

Mrs Rhodes nodded, clearly disinterested. 'I serve breakfast at six and dinner at five. Would you like to see your room?'

It was at the top of the stairs, overlooking the main street. A high, narrow bed with a white chenille coverlet dominated a small space. Mrs Rhodes had also managed to cram a comfortable chair, a washstand, and a hatstand into the small room.

'Very nice,' Tisdale murmured. 'How quiet is it at night?'

'Oh, very.'

'There are no children staying here, by any chance?' he ventured, hoping that there was one small girl.

She cocked her head to the side. 'Of course not, Mr Tisdale. I don't allow children here. They can be very messy.'

'There were children in the last place, and they kept me up half the night, getting up to run around the halls while their parents slept the sleep of the innocent,' Tisdale elaborated.

'Disgraceful,' was all Mrs Rhodes would offer him as she moved down the hall toward the stairs. A door opened down the hall and the man Tisdale thought was Cannon stepped out. Tisdale turned around as if he were taking one last look at the room. He hoped to avoid coming face-to-face with the man, at least until Birch got here.

'Oh, Mr Cutter. Will you be dining with us this evening?' Mrs Rhodes asked.

'Yes, ma'am. I plan on making it an early night. I had a long ride today.'

'I'm roasting a chicken and making a Yorkshire pudding to go with it.' She turned to Tisdale. 'Oh, Mr Cutter, this is Mr Tisdale. He's renting this room for the night.'

Tisdale had no choice but to turn around and offer his hand. Cutter seemed unhappy. Before Tisdale had left Deadwood, Dane had given him a wanted poster that he'd had made up, along with the only other photograph of Hannah. Marie had given the most recent picture of their little girl to Birch.

Dane had taken no chances, describing Cannon in detail to Tisdale. 'Ever since a man cut him in a fight about ten years ago, Cannon's worn a beard to hide the scar, but we were all aware that it was there,' his friend had told him. 'I'll bet that he's shaved it off to change his look, though. It's what I would do.'

And Hal Dane had been right. The scar was prominent, and the white skin surrounding it made it clear that Cutter, or Cannon, had shaved recently.

The two men eyed each other warily, then shook hands. Cannon's hand was strong and rough. Tisdale wondered what had happened to his goddaughter. For a moment, he wanted

73

to end the charade and beat the living daylights out of the man, beat the information out of him. But he knew that for all his righteous indignation, he was still no match for Cannon's brawn.

'Well, I got to get back to my room,' Cutter muttered.

'See you at dinner tonight,' Tisdale called after the man.

Mrs Rhodes took Tisdale's arm and led him toward the stairs again. 'I just knew that you two men would get along. Mr Cutter's here to buy a gold stake as well. You'll have plenty to talk about at dinner tonight. Now, let me show you the dining room, and then we'll take care of the other details.'

Tisdale let her lead him downstairs. He tried to remain interested in what Mrs Rhodes was telling him, but he couldn't keep his mind on the conversation. When she told him how much it was for a room for the night, he didn't quibble over the inflated price.

When he was finally settled in his room, he took the photograph and the wanted poster out of his bag and checked it against his memory of the man he had just met, the man who called himself Cutter. He was certain that Cannon and Cutter were one and the same.

Tisdale wondered if Birch had reached Yellow Jacket yet, and if he had received the wire. He knew Birch's action would depend on how strong the lead was that he was already following. Tisdale knew he would have to be prepared to follow Cannon without Birch's help. He briefly considered wiring Hal Dane, but knew that that would be disastrous.

Tisdale wasn't sure how long he could keep an eye on Cannon without drawing suspicion, and he wondered where Hannah could be. And if she was still alive.

CHAPTER TWELVE

'Are you feeling tired and listless before the sun is up? Do you feel aches and pains that weren't there a year ago? Have you been told that your blood is thin? All of this can be cured with Doc Henry's Patented Miracle Indian Cure. A dime a bottle, two for fifteen cents.' Doc Henry stood on a small platform that had been specially built to attach to the back of the wagon. Three women and one man stood around the back of the wagon, barely listening to Doc. Mary stood quietly to one side and handed a bottle to Doc. With a flourish, he pulled the cork out and took a delicate sip.

'A little can do a lot,' he said before taking a longer swig. 'A lot can do more. You too can be as healthy as the young Indian lady who stands beside me. Let the secret Indian herbs and roots do for you what they have done for her and her ancestors.' He pounded his chest with one hand to show that he was feeling energy coursing through his body.

Birch stood across the street, leaning up against an empty hitching post, listening to Doc Henry's empty words.

He looked up the street, wondering which saloon might be the best place for information when he caught sight of a deputy walking toward Doc Henry's medicine wagon. Maybe he could get some answers or suggestions from him.

'You planning to stay long?' the deputy was asking Doc. 'No, sir,' Doc replied humbly. 'Mary and I will just do one show here, and one this afternoon at the other end of town, then we'll be on our way. If that's fine with you, of course.'

The deputy's chest swelled and he rested his hand protectively on his gunbelt. Birch sensed that this was a man who needed to prove he was the better man. He admired Doc's handling of the situation—it was clear that Doc was adept at reading people. Mary was busy handing out bottles and collecting money from a growing crowd.

Doc reached over and grabbed a bottle of his medicine, handing it to the deputy. 'With my compliments to the fine lawmen here in Yellow Jacket.' The deputy took the bottle, uncorked it, sniffed, and took a tentative sip, then a bigger sip.

Birch approached the deputy and

introduced himself, explaining why he was in Yellow Jacket. Between sips of the medicine, the deputy nodded his head slowly. 'I remember a man and a girl, or maybe it was a boy, passing through here the other day. He had a beard and they traveled in a buckboard. I think they were going north toward a Ute village about twenty miles from here.'

Doc and Mary were packing up their wagon. Birch turned to them. 'I'll be on my way.'

'Thanks for your help yesterday,' Doc said. 'We'd probably still be there if you hadn't come along.'

Mary was suddenly at Doc's side. He leaned down and she talked to him in a low voice, gesturing toward Birch. Doc straightened up and said, 'She told me that she hopes you find the girl. You've probably been told that many times before.'

'I think a lot of people are praying for her safe return,' Birch replied.

Mary said something else to Doc. 'She says that if you find this man, remember that he has suffered a tragedy and probably isn't aware of the suffering he's causing the girl.'

Birch looked at Mary and took her hands in his. 'Tell her that I think she has great wisdom and a warm heart.'

When he had taken leave of Doc and Mary, Birch headed for the telegraph office. A wire from Tisdale was waiting. Birch took it outside to read: FOUND CANNON STOP NO HANNAH

77

STOP MEET IN REDMESA STOP HURRY STOP TISDALE.

It took a moment for Birch to get over the fact that the man he had been following might not, in fact, be Stu Cannon. He had spent the better part of the two days, just a day from, just hours from, coming face-to-face with a man and a little girl. Now he had to ask himself why the man had stopped in Durango for a pair of scissors and boys' clothes, why he had cut his little girl's hair and made her dress like a boy.

Birch was in a dilemma. If Cannon didn't have Hannah, that meant she was somewhere else, with someone else. If he left for Redmesa now and didn't follow up his lead, he might be letting the man who had Hannah slip through his fingers. If the man he was following was in collusion with Cannon, he deserved to be brought in for trial just as Cannon should be brought in.

He decided to spend one more day on his lead, go to the Ute village, see what was going on. From there, he could cut down to Redmesa, get there within a day if he rode all night. Birch felt time running out for Hannah and for reuniting her with her family. He intended to do everything possible to find her, even if it meant going without sleep.

Half an hour later, Birch was heading north toward the Ute village. He had been told that it was twenty miles away, over twin hills that were pointed out to him in the distance. The

78

trail wound around hillocks and small lakes in the middle of nowhere. Farther out, he passed a ranch that consisted of weary-looking buildings and a few horses in a corral.

By early afternoon, Birch had reached the foothills. The trail rose slightly, and snaked between the hills through gaps so narrow at times that Birch's shoulders brushed the sides. The sun was low in the sky when Birch finally reached the Ute village. The Utes looked as if they had gone through a particularly hard winter: the children's ribs were prominent and the women's cheekbones were hollow. The tepees were reinforced with brush to keep the cold from creeping into their living spaces during the winter.

Outside, two young women were preparing a meal, three older women were watching the children play, and several men sat on the edge of the communal area, stringing bows and sharpening hatchets. When Birch rode into the camp, everyone stopped doing what they were doing and stared at him with open hostility.

Dismounting from Cactus, Birch found himself alone. The children and women had retreated to their teepees. Some of the children's bright, curious eyes peered around the teepee flaps.

The chief emerged from his teepee. It was a dwelling that befitted him, decorated and covered with elaborate beading and feather work. The chief was tall, for a Ute, and had noble features. He wore a rabbit-fur cape and rabbit-skin moccasins. A younger Ute accompanied him to greet Birch. Birch tried to read their expressions, but found it impossible.

The younger Ute spoke tersely in broken English. 'This is our chief, Raven Feather. I am called Sharp Claw.'

He turned stiffly and beckoned Birch to join them by the cooking fire. Chief Raven Feather spoke through Sharp Claw. 'We have weapons, and will not hesitate to use them if you are here on a mission for the white men. We have been told we would be given water, and we were given dust in its place. Speak the truth and we will deal with you in kind.'

Birch nodded. The Utes had been dealt a particularly hard deal recently. When silver was discovered on their land, the U.S. Government had moved them, promising to provide rations and good land in trade. Instead, the Utes had been given a small parcel of land, hardly enough to sustain their tribes, and the promised rations had never materialized.

'I am here on a mission that has nothing to do with the government,' Birch explained. 'I am here to find a small girl who was taken away by force from her family.'

'And you blame us for that?' Sharp Claw asked bitterly. He started to get up, drawing his hunting knife. Chief Raven Feather spoke rapidly to Sharp Claw in Ute. Sharp Claw responded in kind. Birch kept his hand casually by his gun in case he was attacked. He had no illusions that he would be treated fairly if they didn't believe him. He knew there was probably at least one rifle aimed at his back; he could almost feel it.

Chief Raven Feather spoke, Sharp Claw translating for Birch. 'It has been a long, barren winter and our bellies are howling. Other white men have given us only empty promises of food and clothing.' Here the chief paused to assess Birch. The tall Texan must have passed some test, because Raven Feather's eyes glanced over to Sharp Claw, and the chief nodded approvingly. 'Now the season of growing has begun, and we rejoice. We will plant seeds and watch food grow. We will hunt for skins and meat, bone and sinew. We will have new clothes to wear, we will have food to eat, and we can repair our dwellings. We have prayed to the Great Spirit for all of this, and it will come to pass.'

A young Ute woman approached with a bowl, which was handed to Chief Raven Feather. He took it and sipped the liquid, then passed it to Birch, who did the same. The drink was slightly sweet. Birch noticed that when he drank from the bowl, the Utes visibly relaxed. Chief Raven Feather even gave a slight nod to Sharp Claw. He spoke again. 'You honor us with your presence. What is the reason for your visit?'

Birch reiterated his reason for riding into their camp. The chief and his young aide listened intently. When Birch was finished, Sharp Claw translated it for his chief. Chief Raven Feather muttered something back, his black eyes focused sharply on Birch.

'There was a man and boy who rode into camp when the sun first rose,' Sharp Claw said. Chief Raven Feather started to talk again. Sharp Claw listened respectfully and translated for Birch. 'My chief wants to tell you that the man wanted to sell the boy to us, but the winter was not good to us, and we do not have the resources to share. The man suggested that the boy would grow up to aid us in hunting. But we could not take the boy.'

Birch nodded. Sharp Claw listened to his chief again, and replied in Ute. Then he turned to Birch and said, 'This man, he has no right to the boy?'

'This man has no right to the child. And the child is not male, but female. The man dressed the girl as a boy.' Birch took out the photo of Hannah and handed it to the chief. Raven Feather and Sharp Claw studied it.

The young Ute looked mystified. 'We do not understand.'

Birch tried to give the Ute chief and his aide some explanation. 'Perhaps the man believes that boys and men have a higher value than girls. Or he might be trying to protect the girl from outlaws in rough country.' He wasn't even sure that this man he was tracking still had Hannah.

Birch thanked the chief and his aide, and set out in the direction that had been pointed out as that of the man and boy. He rode Cactus hard, intending to make up for lost time. If he was reading Sharp Claw's information correctly, 'when the sun first rose' meant early this morning. That meant that the man was traveling at a slower pace than Birch, having no idea that he was being pursued. This also did not sit well with Birch: If this man was Cannon, or was an accomplice of Cannon's, why hadn't he gotten rid of Hannah sooner?

It was late afternoon when Birch caught up with his quarry. They rode in a buckboard with one wobbly wheel and creaking axles. Pulling the wagon was an old, tired horse.

'Whoa,' Birch commanded the buggy's horse, pulling up alongside and taking the reins.

'What're you up to, mister?' the man said, his voice filled with suspicion. 'If you're trying to rob us, I got to warn you that we're dirt poor.'

Birch got off Cactus and drew his gun. The driver, a thin, wiry man with dirty blond hair, put his hands in the air to show he had no gun. Seeing no sign of the girl up front, Birch inspected the back, finally finding the young child under a tarpaulin playing with a corncob doll. The youngster looked up at him with wide

83

eyes, not saying a word. Even without checking the photograph in his pocket, Birch knew this wasn't Hannah.

Still, he asked tentatively, 'Hannah?'

The child stared at him with an expressionless face. If he hadn't known about the scissors and the boys' clothes, he would think that this child was a little boy.

Birch felt a hand on his shoulder. 'Hey, what do you think you're—' the man never finished his question. Out of frustration and instinct, Birch turned around and clipped the man's jaw. He fell back to the ground, staring up at the sky, stunned. A moment later, he pulled himself up to his elbows and began to rub his jaw. 'What'd you do that for, stranger?'

For the first time since he had caught up with this wagon, Birch could see that the man he had punched looked nothing like Stu Cannon, not the way he had been described to Birch. He also had no scar on his neck.

Tension seemed to drain away from Birch and he slumped against the wagon. 'You're not Stu Cannon,' he said.

'Damn right,' the man said, carefully getting up as he eyed Birch's gunbelt. 'You can have anything you want, mister, just leave me and my own alone. Just don't shoot us.'

Birch shook his head. 'I'm not going to use it. I'm not here to rob you.' He frowned. 'You say that this child is yours, but I just came from the Ute camp. They tell me that you tried to sell

84

the child to them. And I know that this is a girl, not a boy.'

The man had the grace to flush and look away. 'Mister, you don't have the right to know anything about me. Before I answer any of your damned questions, you answer a few for me. What've you been doing, following me like this and asking all them questions?'

Birch figured this was fair enough. He explained in as few words as possible. 'That sounds like a right terrible situation,' the man replied when Birch was finished. 'The name's Elijah Brand. This here's little Elmore.'

He caught sight of Birch's raised brows. 'Yes, Elmore's a boy, all right. And considerin' what you've put yourself through to catch up to me, I got to tell you straight out that you've been followin' the wrong trail. And I'm sorry our paths crossed. Sorry for you that you been chasin' wild geese.'

The air was getting chilly and the sun was going down. Elijah looked around for a moment, then reached up and pulled his boy from the wagon. 'Looks like as good a spot to set up camp as any.'

Birch helped Elmore gather firewood, and they soon had a cheery fire going. Sensing that the Brands didn't have a lot of worldly goods in their wagon, Birch shared his supplies with them. Coffee was soon boiling in a battered pot and Elmore was gnawing on pemmican and hardtack.

'Thanks for the grub, Mr Birch,' Elijah said, taking a sliver to clean his teeth. Elmore moved closer to his father. 'I guess I owe you an explanation before you get on your way. Five years ago, my wife, Beth, and I had a little girl. Her name was Elizabeth. Lizzie we called her. But she died of the fever one winter, the winter before Elmore was born. My wife, God bless her, was a good woman, but Lizzie's death was too much of a strain on her. Beth began to pine for her little girl and by the time Elmore was born, she had decided that our new baby was Lizzie. She dressed Elmore in girl clothes, she called him Lizzie, and she made him play with dolls.' Elijah looked over at his boy, sorrow evident in his eyes. He sighed. 'I tell you, Mr Birch, it's been a trial for me, and no good for my boy. Beth died last week. She went wandering where she shouldn't've gone and fell into a ravine. Since then, it's just been me and the boy. I decided to sell the homestead and start a new life. I'm starting to treat Elmore like the boy he is, and hope I can undo some of the damage caused by my poor, addled Beth.'

They fell silent for awhile. Birch added a branch to the fire. 'Why did you try to sell Elmore to the Utes?'

Elijah's eyes closed. 'A man sometimes reaches the end of his rope, and I guess this morning, I reached mine. I got scared thinking about Elmore and what his mama done to him.

And I began to think that it was my fault. If I'd've stood up to Beth, if I'd've done something about her nervous condition sooner, maybe things would have been better for Elmore. I thought maybe he'd be better off with the Indians, that's what I thought. And I thought, maybe I can get a little stake, get some supplies for moving on; I'd be out of Elmore's life, and he could learn about being a man from them Indians.' Elijah shook his head, running his hand across the back of his neck. 'It was a crazy thought, but I thought I'd save Elmore from me.'

Birch wasn't sure he totally believed Elijah, but he had to take the man at his word. He didn't know the situation. The little boy had been solemn and silent the whole time Birch had been with them. The agent had enough problems trying to track one little girl without adding the problems of this small boy to his agenda. He regretted having to leave without checking out Elijah's story, but he had no choice. As he took his leave of the father and son, Birch wondered what would become of the sad little Elmore, whose mama had treated him like a girl and whose daddy was ashamed of him.

CHAPTER THIRTEEN

Tisdale pushed back from the table, feeling slow and heavy from the large breakfast of eggs, biscuits, and pepper gravy.

'Are you sure you won't have the last egg, Mr Tisdale?' Mrs Rhodes asked, extending the platter toward him.

Tisdale held up a hand. 'No, thank you. It was delicious.'

'Will you be staying another night?'

'I'm not sure.'

Mrs Rhodes turned to Cannon, who was still mopping up his egg with a piece of fried bread. 'And you, Mr Cutter. Will you be staying here another night?'

Tisdale held his breath, hoping that Cannon would say yes. Cannon paused, then shook his head. Tisdale's heart sank. 'Can't. Gotta head south,' was all Cannon said before resuming his meal.

Tisdale excused himself and went up to his room to pack his things. He would have to trail Cannon himself, but he also had to find a way to leave a message for Birch. The most likely place would be the telegraph office. He hoped he would have the time. At least he knew that Cannon was heading south.

Tisdale thanked Mrs Rhodes once more before taking his leave. He saddled his horse and made a detour to leave a message at the telegraph office, then went back to the boardinghouse. Cannon was already hitching his horse to the buckboard. Tisdale hung back behind a tree and waited. A few minutes later, he watched Cannon drive his wagon out of Redmesa, heading south.

Tisdale knew it would be suspicious if he just hung back and tried to follow at a distance. The land was so unpredictable that while that might work in hilly or mountainous areas, it wouldn't work on the flat plains. He pushed his horse to catch up and drew alongside Cannon's wagon.

'You heading south?'

Cannon eyed Tisdale warily. 'That's right.'

'Mind some company?' Tisdale asked, adding, 'I don't like traveling alone in this country. There's a lot of bandits out there.'

Cannon seemed to think about it for a minute, then gave a short nod. 'All right. Just don't expect much from me. I like to be alone.'

The uneasy truce being drawn, they rode in silence for a while. Finally, Tisdale ventured to ask some questions. 'Where exactly are you heading?'

'New Mexico,' was Cannon's answer.

'Any particular town?'

Cannon shot a look at Tisdale. 'I told you I don't like to talk much. Let's just leave it at that.'

Tisdale fell silent again. By the time the sun

had climbed up the clear blue sky, Tisdale was hungry again. Cannon had several beef dodgers, which Mrs Rhodes must have made for him the night before. Tisdale eyed Cannon's corn-and-minced-beef cakes, hoping that Cannon would offer one to him, but he watched Cannon polish them off by himself. Tisdale chewed his dry, tasteless crackers and chipped beef. His canteen water had a metallic taste that did nothing to relieve his thirst. He wished he'd thought to stop by a saloon and fill up the waterskin with an ale cocktail. The combination of ale, ginger, and pepper was a favorite on a summer's day in San Francisco.

Cannon drank from his own waterskin, the smell of whiskey unmistakable to Tisdale.

'Is New Mexico where you hail from?' Tisdale asked Cannon. He figured that even though Cannon had said he didn't want to talk, they couldn't spend the entire day in silence. He was also hoping to get more of an idea of what Cannon was planning, hoping that he might slip in some information that would lead to Hannah.

'Nope,' was all Cannon said. He took another swig of water.

'Then you must come from Colorado.'

Cannon glared at him. 'Why all the questions?'

'Just making conversation.'

'Then let's talk about you,' Cannon replied, leaning forward so his elbow rested on his

90

knee. 'Where are you from?'

'California. San Francisco.'

'What're you doin' around here?'

'I'm,' Tisdale hesitated, not sure what story he had told the woman at the boardinghouse. Had she talked to Cannon about him? Cannon seemed on fairly good terms with her. Tisdale got the impression that Cannon had been staying there for a few nights. The story finally came back to him, full-blown. 'I'm in land speculation.'

'A land man, huh?' When Cannon said this, there was disgust in his tone. 'If you're so good at land speculation, why are you heading south? Everyone knows that the best land is in Colorado and Oklahoma right now. New Mexico is a wasteland.' Cannon jerked the reins and the wagon crept forward.

Tisdale eased his horse down to a walk. He tried to sound authoritative. 'That's what they want you to think. But if you remember, silver and gold were found in New Mexico and Arizona about twenty years ago. Then there was the trouble with the Indians and, well, exploration was held up.'

Cannon glanced at Tisdale, a glint of curiosity and greed in his eyes. 'You really think so?'

Tisdale was starting to enjoy his new role, but he was mindful of overplaying his hand. 'Well, I've said too much already. Just keep what I've said under your hat.'

He had started something. 'I've never been to New Mexico before,' Cannon said.

'I was there once about a year ago. Albuquerque.' That much was true. The Sante Fe Railroad had hired Tisdale Investigations to catch a train robber. Tisdale had called in Birch, who went after the man, albeit reluctantly. 'If you think Colorado is hot, wait till you get to New Mexico. My advice is to stay near the Rio Grande. The towns are more plentiful, and you're always near water,' Tisdale added. 'What kind of work are you looking for?'

'I don't know,' Cannon replied dully. 'I used to own a saloon. But I don't think I can go back to it.'

'Why not?'

Cannon looked sharply at Tisdale as if he were weighing his answer. 'Your place is just target practice for every crazy who thinks he's the next Billy the Kid or some other well-known gun.' He looked straight ahead and added, 'Besides, my family's gone now. Don't need a stake in some place that keeps me tied down.' Cannon used the reins to urge on his horse a little faster. The day was not uncomfortable. A slight cool breeze blew across the land. Tisdale noticed that the land was becoming less hilly, flatter. As they neared the New Mexico border, the lushness turned to lifelessness. The colors of the landscape were muted, no longer the hopeful green of spring.

'Do you know what the first town is called?'

Cannon took his time answering. 'Flora Vista. We'll be there in time to get a room and dinner.'

Tisdale was finding it hard to believe that he almost liked Cannon. He wasn't an easy traveling companion, and it was obvious to Tisdale that even if he hadn't known the man's recent past, Cannon wore tragedy and defeat like an albatross.

He hated what Cannon had done. Abducting Hannah was unconscionable, regardless of his reason. And for all Tisdale knew, Cannon had already killed the child or left her for dead somewhere. Tisdale fervently wished that he hadn't initiated a conversation with Cannon because he preferred hating the image of evil he had been pursuing. Getting to know Cannon man-to-man made investigating more difficult for Tisdale, who was unaccustomed to doing clandestine fieldwork. He wanted things to be the way they had been before he left Redmesa. He had been blissfully ignorant and had blindly followed the clues that might lead him to Hannah.

CHAPTER FOURTEEN

Flora Vista had one rooming house in town, and it had only one available room.

93

'If you boys don't mind sharing,' the owner, Mrs Simmons, suggested, 'I have one room with two beds in it.' She had a military quality about her. Her bearing was stiff, and it was clear to Tisdale that she wasn't at all shy about evicting the man who occupied the two-bed room, sending him to a smaller room with one bed. But at least they had a place to sleep that night.

The problem was that Tisdale wasn't sure he could sleep in the same room with Cannon. And it appeared that Cannon was resistant to the idea as well. The only thing that seemed to mollify Cannon was the slightly lower than usual rate that the owner offered for the inconvenience.

Tisdale couldn't understand why Cannon was staying in Flora Vista in the first place. He had a buckboard, he could have slept in it somewhere along the trail. Tisdale needed to find out what was keeping Cannon here in Flora Vista.

After bringing their belongings up to their room, Cannon left, disappearing down the street as Tisdale watched from a window that looked out on the main thoroughfare. Tisdale had no way of following him without making it obvious, so he went to the telegraph office and sent a wire to Birch, care of Redmesa. If Birch hadn't arrived in Redmesa yet, he would have two messages waiting for him.

Night crept slowly into the town of Flora

Vista. Tisdale went to a restaurant and had steak and tortillas, then wandered over to a saloon across the street from the rooming house.

It was a lively place for such a small town. Saloon girls sat on men's laps and enticed customers to buy them drinks. Tisdale frequently witnessed several women's free hands reaching down to the sacks of gold dust tucked into men's waistbands.

He was working on his third whiskey, ruminating on sneaking back to the room to have a look at Cannon's personal belongings, when a dark-eyed woman approached him. She wore her black hair long and straight, with a white flower tucked behind her ear. Cheap perfume assaulted him, making his eyes water and his nostrils twitch. She sat in an empty chair next to him.

'You are perhaps looking for someone to talk to?' she asked in a sultry, exotic voice. 'My name is Concetta.'

Olga, Tisdale's fiancée back in San Francisco, would not approve of this type of woman. Concetta's cheeks were painted, and she wore a purple dress that revealed her charms for the world to see. Olga frowned upon flamboyant dresses and face paint.

There were times when Tisdale thought Olga could use a little fixing up in both areas, but she was a good woman and he knew he was lucky to have her. She did have that fine, porcelain skin that most Scandinavians seemed to inherit, her blue eyes were wide and sparkled when she laughed, and her cheekbones were high, making her blush prettily when he paid her a compliment.

'Hello, Concetta,' Tisdale replied, noticing that he was slurring his words slightly. It was time to slow down on his drinking. 'And I suppose you'd like a drink for your time.'

She chuckled. 'What is talk without a drink in a place like this?'

He placed a couple of coins on the table between them, and a moment later, another girl set two glasses and a bottle before them. Tisdale poured a generous shot for Concetta, aware that his hand shook slightly. But he prided himself on not spilling a drop.

'You look like a kind man,' Concetta said, then quickly knocked back her drink. She held out her glass for another shot. Tisdale poured. At the rate she drank, he'd be broke in a few minutes. 'Are you just passing through?'

'I'm staying at the rooming house for the night,' Tisdale admitted.

'Then you might be around for a few days,' Concetta said. She leaned forward and put her hand on his thigh. Tisdale jumped. She leered and giggled. 'Maybe we can have some fun while you're here. How long do you plan to stay?'

'I—I don't know. I could be here a week, or I might leave tomorrow.'

'Oh, a drifter,' she said with a wink.

Tisdale caught sight of a familiar face across the smoky saloon. Stu Cannon had walked in and was leaning against the bar. Concetta squeezed Tisdale's thigh to remind him of her presence. 'What is it?' she asked, her eyes narrowing. 'Do you see a girl you like better? I am the jealous type, you know.'

'Miss,' Tisdale replied, giving her only half his attention. He had just had an idea. 'Concetta. How would you like to make some money?'

Her eyes and her smile widened. 'Mister, you said the right thing.' She held out her hand, palm up.

Tisdale counted out a generous sum. When she had tucked the money in the purse she kept in her waistband, Concetta became all business. 'Now. Tell me what I must do.'

He pointed Cannon out to her. 'See that man? Do you think you can keep him busy for about half an hour?'

She stood up and faced Tisdale. 'What do you think? Can I distract a man for half an hour?' Concetta smiled, wriggled her hips, blew Tisdale a kiss, and headed for her quarry.

Tisdale watched for about five minutes, enough time to make sure that Concetta's charms were not missed by Cannon. When he was satisfied, he slipped out of the saloon and back to the rooming house. As he crept up the stairs, a strident voice called out from the bottom of the stairs. 'Oh, Mr Tisdale, how has your evening been? You must be turning in for the night.'

Tisdale turned around to face Mrs Simmons. She looked different, more relaxed. He noticed the half-full glass in her hand and realized that she had been drinking. She started up the stairs, trying to maintain a dignity that was altogether gone by the time she stumbled on the third step. Tisdale, afraid she'd fall and break her neck, descended quickly and helped her back down to the hall.

'Oh, you're so kind,' she trilled, looking up at him and batting her eyelashes. 'Won't you join me for a drink?'

Tisdale glanced longingly up the stairs. 'Well, I'm really quite tired—'

'It gets so lonely here sometimes,' Mrs Simmons continued, as if she hadn't heard a word he'd said. 'I cook and clean and try to retain some order to this place, but it's so hard to do it all alone.' She trailed off, and Tisdale was about to disengage himself politely from this one-way conversation when she continued, 'Are you all alone, Mr Tisdale? I know you're not what you seem.'

Alarmed, Tisdale asked cautiously, 'I'm not?'

'Oh, no.' She waved her hand in the air dismissively, wobbling slightly. Tisdale steered her toward the parlor, where he deposited her on a wingbacked chair. 'When you took the room with that other man this afternoon, you told me you were a land speculator, and that you're looking for stakes to sell to investors out in the east. You told me you were happy, but I can tell that what you need is a good woman.' She emphasized her point by leaning forward and attempting to give him a meaningful look. It turned into more of a leer.

'Would you like another brandy, Mrs Simmons?' Tisdale got up and took the nearly empty glass from her hand.

'Oh, you are a gentleman,' she said, giggling.

He went over to her decanters, which were by a window that looked out on the main street. While he poured, he glanced out to see if he still had time. There was no sign of Cannon coming toward the rooming house. He turned back to her. 'There. I've got a nice big glass—' He stopped talking as he realized that she had fallen asleep. She must have had more to drink than he'd realized. She snorted once as he quietly set the brandy glass down on the table in front of her and left the parlor.

Time was short, and Tisdale took the stairs two at a time. It took only a few minutes to go through his roommate's personal belongings, and he found what he was looking for in a small box. At least, he thought it might be something, but he couldn't tell yet what it was because it was wrapped in brown paper and tied securely with string, obviously ready to be sent by mail somewhere. There was no address on it yet, but there was a name: Hannah. Tisdale felt the package give—whatever was inside was soft. He was getting ready to open it carefully when he heard the sound of heavy footsteps coming down the hallway.

Stuffing the package back in the box and putting things back where he'd found them, Tisdale thought quickly. He turned down the lamp wick, kicked off his boots and stripped off his trousers and shirt, tossing them carelessly on the wooden straightbacked chair in the corner. Not a moment too soon, he slipped between the rough sheets of his bed and rolled over on his side, breathing noisily to make Cannon think he was asleep.

Tisdale heard the doorknob turn, then light from the hall spilled into the darkened room. Cannon's shadow blocked out the light for a split second, then the door quietly closed. The floorboards creaked as Cannon made his way across the dark room. Concetta's cheap fragrance assaulted Tisdale's nose and he knew that the saloon girl he had paid had done well.

He just wished he'd found the package with Hannah's name on it sooner, or that Concetta had been able to distract Cannon for a few minutes longer. He might have discovered what was so important that Cannon had wrapped it in brown paper and had started to address it.

Before drifting off to sleep, Tisdale wondered if Cannon would be staying here in town another night, or if he would pack up and leave tomorrow. He knew he couldn't keep this pretense up much longer. Cannon would become suspicious if Tisdale tried to accompany him. He would have to take his chances and follow Cannon at a distance if he left tomorrow.

He hoped Birch had gotten the wire and was riding toward Flora Vista tonight. What would be even better was if Birch had already found Hannah. But Tisdale had his doubts about ever finding Hannah, unless Cannon led them to her. It was a big country, and he'd picked up the trail too late.

He wondered what Cannon had been like before his son shot a man in cold blood and was hanged. He thought he understood the pain Cannon must have gone through. It was funny how things worked out. Tisdale knew that Birch's wife had died in childbirth, but his agent and friend hadn't let the tragedy turn him into a bitter man. Cannon, on the other hand, had allowed his tragedy to twist him inside.

Tisdale hoped that if they never found Hannah, Cannon had had the decency to leave her with people who would take good care of her. And he hoped that Hal Dane wouldn't become another Stu Cannon.

When Tisdale woke up the next morning, weak daylight crept cautiously through the curtains of the one window. Tisdale looked over at the other bed. Cannon was already gone, bags and all. It took a moment to seep into his brain, and when it did, Tisdale bolted out of bed as if struck by lightning and dressed as fast as he could. Grabbing his hastily packed saddlebags, he clattered down the stairs and almost collided with Mrs Simmons.

'Hang on a moment,' she said genially, 'breakfast is just being put on the table. No need to hurry.'

'Mr Cannon,' Tisdale replied, then remembering that he was using a different name, 'Mr Cutter. Have you seen him?'

'Why yes,' Mrs Simmons said slowly, too slowly for Tisdale, 'he left in his buckboard. Didn't seem interested in a meal before he left, although he took a couple of my corn cakes for later. Glad to give them to him. Some of these fellas who come in are in a real hurry to—'

Tisdale didn't wait to hear the rest. He didn't even grab a couple of biscuits or corn cakes. He just thanked her and made his exit.

He still had to saddle his horse, the skittish gray mare that Dane had loaned him for his journey. After several attempts, Tisdale finally got the mare saddled, climbed on, and rode out of Flora Vista. The land south of town opened up to him; a sweeping valley of wildflowers, paintbrush, bistort, and buttercups were beginning to reveal their colors.

Tisdale continued the descent into the valley. He could see a shepherd and his sheep in the distance. A dog romped around the edges of the flock, keeping a watchful eye on any sheep that might stray.

After fifteen minutes of riding into the valley, Tisdale stopped his mare and peered around, looking for signs of Cannon. Yesterday, he remembered Cannon telling him that he was heading south. And driving a buckboard, well, he couldn't have gotten very far. He certainly couldn't have crossed the valley by now.

The click of a hammer being cocked behind him caused Tisdale to hold his breath.

'Well, now,' said a familiar voice, 'this is just dandy. You lookin' for someone, Mr Tisdale?'

Cannon. Tisdale closed his eyes. 'What's going on?' he asked in an even tone of voice. 'Is that you, Cutter?'

'It's me, but my name ain't Cutter,' Cannon said. 'And I think you know that.'

Tisdale turned around slowly. 'I don't know what you're talking about. I'm here looking at the land.'

Cannon was on his horse, the buckboard nowhere in sight. 'I think you know exactly who I am. I asked the local assayer's office, and they hadn't heard of you. All land men go to an assayer to find out what land's still available and what land's already been taken.'

Stupid of me, Tisdale thought. 'All right, I know you're Stu Cannon and you took an innocent little girl from her family. Tell me

103

where she is. All Hal Dane wants is Hannah. I'll make sure he doesn't go after you.'

Cannon shook his head. 'No, I've gone too far now. I can't go back.'

A sick feeling overwhelmed Tisdale, as if he were about to throw up. 'You mean, you murdered her, you son of a bitch?' he managed to whisper.

Cannon looked impatient. 'No. I couldn't do it. Even though Dane is as responsible for murdering my boy as the hangman. I couldn't do it. Let's just say that Dane will never see his precious little girl again.'

The faint sound of pounding hooves caught the attention of both men. Tisdale caught a glimpse of Birch astride Cactus, at the crest of the valley. He knew he had to distract Cannon.

'What about the package?'

He had gotten Cannon's attention. 'The package?'

'Last night, while you were still in the saloon, I took the liberty of going through your bags. I saw a brown paper package addressed to Hannah.'

Cannon gave him a black look at first, then grinned. 'Ah, yes. That package is safely on its way to Hannah now. She left her rag doll in the buckboard. I found someone who was going in the direction Hannah is, and I sent the package with him.'

'What do you intend to do with me?' Tisdale asked.

He knew there was no distracting Cannon now. Birch had Cactus galloping full tilt toward Cannon. Cannon craned his neck around, then aimed his weapon at Birch. Before he could pull the trigger, Birch swung his arm up and knocked Cannon off his horse. Cannon's gun fell hard to the ground and went off, scaring the horses. Tisdale's mare reared up, but he managed to stay on and get her under control while Cannon's horse ran down into the valley. Cactus capered nervously as Birch slid out of the saddle.

Tisdale jumped off his horse to help Birch overpower Cannon. As he watched the two men struggle on the rocky incline, Tisdale realized that he would have to wait for the right opportunity. Birch slugged Cannon in the jaw, slamming him onto his back. Cannon rolled onto his stomach, getting up on his hands and knees. He staggered getting up onto his feet and flung himself at Birch.

When they toppled to the ground again, Cannon straddling Birch, his hands around Birch's neck, Tisdale picked up a sizable rock and started toward them. But before he had a chance to hit Cannon from behind, Birch had gained the upper hand and had kicked Cannon off.

Tisdale hovered on the edge of the fight, waiting for his chance. Then he spied Cannon's gun. As he headed toward it, Cannon managed to break away from Birch and make a dash for the gun. He reached it first, picked it up, and aimed it at Tisdale. Tisdale froze.

'No!' Birch shouted. Tisdale closed his eyes and listened to the sound of two shots being fired in close succession. He expected to feel the fiery sting of a bullet, but when he opened his eyes, he witnessed Cannon clutching his side, his gun dropping from his hand. In slow motion, he fell to the ground and lay there with limbs splayed.

CHAPTER FIFTEEN

Birch stood there, his Navy Colt smoking in his hand. He had never shot a man in the back before, but it was the only way to save Tisdale. If he'd been closer, he might have been able to aim to wound instead of kill. Even now, as Birch stood over the dying man, it was clear to him that bitterness and hate had been the only thing keeping Cannon alive. He seemed to enjoy every breath as an ultimate revenge on Hal Dane—he would die without making any peace, and he would allow an innocent child to grow up never realizing where to find her real family.

Birch felt Tisdale's shoulder roughly brush past as he knelt over Cannon and tried to staunch the blood leaking from his sternum. 'Cannon,' Tisdale said, desperation clear in his voice, 'you're dying. You've had your revenge. Tell us where the child is. It could make all the difference in where you're going from this life.'

Cannon winced. Blood trickled out of the corner of his mouth and uncertainty lined his face. For just a moment, Birch thought Tisdale had gotten to him. Then Cannon broke into a smile. He chuckled. 'Heaven or hell, huh?' Cannon gasped, coughing up more blood. 'I guess I'll take hell. At least that way I get to see my boy again.'

'Are you so hard-hearted? You're punishing a little girl for a crime she didn't commit,' an impassioned Tisdale said.

Birch stood by silently, knowing that it was no use. Cannon was a man who had gone too far to find his way back.

Tisdale sat back on his heels, Birch watching impassively over his employer's shoulder, as Cannon twitched and the death rattle sounded. In a moment, Stu Cannon's empty shell stared up at the sun, unblinking. Tisdale sat motionless. It was Birch who bent over the body and closed his victim's eyes.

Tisdale got up and brushed dirt off his knees. 'Well, I guess that's the end of the trail.' He didn't look at Birch. A drawn-out silence followed, unsaid things hovering painfully between them. 'I don't blame you, you know.'

Birch nodded. 'All the same, I'm sorry it ended this way.' During the search for Hannah, he had begun to feel close to this little

107

girl he had never set eyes on. Birch had even started to feel hopeful that he would find her. Now, that prospect seemed doubtful. 'If I'd been closer, I could have winged him.'

Tisdale clapped a hand on Birch's shoulder. 'You did the best you could. I might have been lying there instead of Cannon if you hadn't shot him.'

Birch holstered his gun and grabbed Cactus's reins. Tisdale's mare had followed the path of Cannon's horse. While Tisdale stayed where he was, Birch rode down to the valley floor to retrieve the two horses. When he came back, Tisdale had a funny look on his face. 'He was driving a buckboard when he left the rooming house in Flora Vista. Where is it now?'

Birch thought about it. 'Maybe he sold it.'

The two men nodded to each other, the same thought running through their heads. They would have to go back to town and find out where Cannon had sold the buckboard. Before doing so, Birch searched Cannon's horse for any clue that might have been left behind. Aside from the bedroll, the saddlebags held only a modest amount of money, several corn cakes, a canteen, and an extra shirt.

As they headed back, Tisdale began to give Birch a report of what had happened the previous night in Flora Vista.

'You roomed with him?' Birch interrupted, trying not to look too impressed. He hadn't thought Tisdale had the imagination or nerve to do what he had done.

'There wasn't much choice,' Tisdale replied modestly. 'By this morning, he had figured out that I wasn't a land man. Cannon became suspicious of me and discovered that I hadn't made the obligatory trip to the assayer's office.' Tisdale's face flushed slightly. 'I guess I'm not much at making up stories.'

'You did the best you could,' Birch replied noncomittally. 'I wouldn't have thought to attach myself to Cannon like that. He would probably have seen me following him, and one of us would have died sooner.'

They were soon on the edge of Flora Vista. 'I regret letting that package slip through my fingers,' Tisdale said.

Birch tugged the reins on Cactus, who slowed down. 'What package?'

Tisdale slowed his mare down and explained about hiring Concetta so he could search Cannon's belongings. 'It was wrapped in brown paper and had Hannah's name on it. When Cannon thought he was going to kill me, he admitted that it was the rag doll Hannah left behind, and that he had sent it on its way with a stranger who was passing through the area where Hannah now lives.'

Birch stared at him. 'That's a lead, Tisdale. You just gave us hope.' He spurred Cactus to a trot, leaving Tisdale to try to catch up.

CHAPTER SIXTEEN

The door to Marshal Darnell Webb's Deadwood office flew open with a bang. A young boy stood in the doorway, out of breath, an envelope in his hand.

'Marshal, the stagecoach just brought the mail. There's a letter for you here.' The boy sprinted across the room to Webb's desk and handed it to the lawman, who was sitting at his desk, drumming his fingers on the blotter surface. Even though he didn't use it, Webb kept a blotter on his desk because he thought it added class to his office. He hated his job, but was hoping that he could run for mayor next term. He thought he was popular enough with the townspeople. Stu Cannon had certainly been a help in getting Webb elected marshal, and they had talked of plans to run against the current mayor. Webb would prefer a position that didn't have anything to do with guns or outlaws, but he couldn't complain about some of the benefits that went along with his job.

He tossed a penny to the boy and smiled. 'Thanks, kid. Go get yourself some candy.'

'Gee thanks, Marshal,' the boy replied, staring at his easily won coin before turning and sprinting out the door.

Webb smiled at the empty doorway, then turned to the letter. It was from Stu Cannon,

110

and it was short and to the point. He had written the letter from a boardinghouse in a town about a day's ride from Deadwood. He wrote that he suspected that he was being followed.

They're closing in on me, but it's too late for them to get what they want. It is also too late for me, my friend. By the time you read this, I will either be well away from here to start a new life, or I will be dead. Whatever happens, this is the last time you will hear from me.
I have one request of you: I do not believe Hal Dane has suffered enough for Hugh's death. I want him to know that what happened to Hannah is his own fault, for what he did to Hugh. Tell him Hannah is still alive, but she's where he will never find her, no matter how long he searches. I wish I could be there to see the look on his face.

Marshal Webb read it through a second time. He remembered when Cannon had come to him about revenge. He had tried to dissuade his friend the way he had tried to dissuade Dane from stirring up the ashes of that drifter's murder. Even when the wife of the drifter pressed Dane for justice, Webb reminded Dane that his duty was to the citizens of Deadwood, not to some woman from out of town. But Dane hadn't listened, and neither had Cannon.

111

Now the whole thing was a mess: Cannon's son was dead, Dane's innocent little girl was missing, and several people's lives had been destroyed. Dane had sent for some friend of his who was an investigator. Webb wondered if this friend was the one following Cannon.

Now he had been asked to do a favor for his friend, the man who was responsible for getting Webb elected. Webb shook his head. He owed Cannon his position as marshal, yet when Cannon had needed him most, Webb hadn't been able to save Hugh from the hangman's noose. He sure as hell could do this favor for Cannon now.

Webb settled back in his chair and thought about ways to get Hal Dane alone. He would have to be clever and cunning. He picked up the *Deadwood Gazette* and his eye was drawn to the engraving of Hannah and the caption that begged the reader's attention. An idea began to form in his mind.

CHAPTER SEVENTEEN

It didn't take long for Birch and Tisdale to find the man who bought the buckboard. Birch was surprised at how quickly Tisdale spotted the wagon outside the livery. He hadn't thought his employer would know one buckboard from another.

'Are you sure this is Cannon's?'

'Yes,' Tisdale replied. 'See the faded red sides? And a spoke is missing from the left front wheel.'

Birch walked up to it and inspected the wheel. 'All the spokes are here,' he called out to Tisdale, who was on the other side of the wagon, peering inside the open back. But as Birch examined each individual spoke more closely, he realized that one of the spokes was newer than the rest.

As he was running his hand over the new spoke, a voice spoke from behind him. 'I just replaced that spoke a few minutes ago.' Birch stood up to face a small, bearded, overweight man. 'Are you interested in buying it?'

Tisdale had come around the side of the wagon to stand by Birch's side. Birch noticed that his employer was holding something.

'I was wondering about the previous owner,' Birch said. The man suddenly looked wary. 'I don't know what you're talking about. I've owned this buckboard for years.'

'If that's the case,' Tisdale spoke up, 'then why was this box in your wagon?' He held up a small leather box.

'Th-th-that's mine!' the man sputtered. 'Put it down right now.'

'What's your name?' Tisdale asked, casually turning the box over in his hands.

'I don't see that it's any business of yours,' the man replied in a contrary tone.

'Humor him,' Birch said in a level voice.

'Osgood, Martin Osgood.'

Tisdale showed the lid of the box to Birch. There was a small brass tag attached to it with the engraved initials S.C.

'If your name is Martin Osgood, why does your box have the initials S.C. on it?' Birch asked.

Osgood's shoulders slumped. He must have been too tired to fabricate another story. 'I bought the buckboard this morning from a stranger passing through town. He said he needed the money more than he needed the wagon, but I had a feeling something was wrong.' Osgood looked up at the two men, resignation and fear in his eyes. 'He seemed nervous. I suspected it was stolen. This is your buckboard, am I right?' Osgood didn't wait for Birch or Tisdale to respond. 'I should have realized right away. I got it for a fraction of what I was willing to pay.'

'And you got all the items in the buckboard as well,' Birch said.

Osgood sighed in a beleaguered manner. 'Yes, he only took the horse and a few possessions from the back. He told me to dispose of the rest as I saw fit. In exchange, I gave him a saddle and blanket.'

'Describe the man,' Birch ordered.

Osgood squeezed his eyes shut. 'Short, a mustache, graying hair.' He opened his eyes and shook his head. 'I didn't pay much attention to him.'

'May we take a look at the things that are left?' Tisdale asked.

Osgood threw up his hands and shook his head. 'It's your buckboard.'

Birch watched Tisdale root through the items—the leather box, a carpet bag, a few tools to repair the wheels or a broken axle, an extra canteen. Tisdale looked up at Osgood, who was quietly creeping away from them. 'Have you removed anything from here?'

The little man stiffened and slowly turned around. 'No. I haven't done anything to the wagon except fix the spoke.' He looked wistfully at the wagon. 'I was going to paint it and give it to my daughter and her new husband. They need a good wagon to get into town from their new ranch.'

Birch looked at Tisdale.

'Was there a brown paper package, perhaps?' Tisdale asked.

'No, I don't remember seeing one.' Osgood frowned. 'He might have taken it with him.' He brightened. 'Or he might have given it to the man he met after our transaction.'

Birch and Tisdale didn't say anything, waiting for Osgood to elaborate, which he did. 'I was inspecting the wheel with the missing spoke and I happened to look up. I saw him meet a man across the street.'

Birch glanced in the direction Osgood was pointing.

Tisdale was still questioning the man. 'Where did they go?'

'Nowhere,' Osgood was saying. 'The other man was ready to leave town. His horse was packed. The man who sold the buckboard to me handed something to the other man, but I didn't see what it was.'

Birch asked Osgood to describe the other man.

'He was about your height,' Osgood said as he looked Birch up and down, 'and had black hair and a beard. It was hard to tell from across the street if he was Mexican, but he wore a black and gray poncho and a slouch hat. If he wasn't Mexican, the way he dressed made me think he might have been down in Mexico recently. He might have been a *vaquero*.'

'What kind of horse did he ride?'

'A pinto.' The man brightened. 'I crossed the street to get a drink and noticed that, when he rode away, the horse had recently been shod.'

It was a good description, more than enough to go on. Osgood also told Birch and Tisdale that the vaquero had headed north, possibly in the direction of Deadwood.

Birch and Tisdale headed for their horses.

'What about the buckboard?' Osgood asked, gesturing to the faded red wagon.

'Keep it,' Tisdale replied.

'You earned it,' Birch added as he wheeled Cactus around and headed north out of town, Tisdale close on his heels.

They rode in silence before coming to a small lake surrounded by a few wind-stunted bristlecone pines. Both men dismounted and led their horses to the edge of the water.

'We should split up,' Birch said, crouching to fill his canteen.

Tisdale nodded. 'I expected as much. Is it possible to find this man described by Osgood?'

'Possible. We've been following his trail for the last hour.'

Out of the corner of his eye, Birch witnessed Tisdale's double take. 'Osgood mentioned that the man's horse had recently been shod.' He got up, knees creaking, and tugged at Cactus's reins to lead him away from the water. Tisdale did the same. When the two men were side by side, Birch stopped and pointed at an impression in the soft ground. 'See that hoofprint?' Tisdale bent over for a closer look. 'That shoe is fairly new. He stopped here to water his horse.'

Tisdale straightened. 'Then we're on the right track.'

Birch nodded. 'If we can trust what Osgood was telling us, and if what Cannon gave the stranger was that package for Hannah.' He turned away and looked at the distant mountains. 'And if he did give this man the package, did he give instructions to take the package to Hannah, wherever she is, or did he just give the package away to a stranger, the same as he practically gave the buckboard away to Osgood?'

Tisdale nodded his understanding, seeming to digest this dilemma. Birch noted the lines around his employer's eyes and mouth, tight, weary lines that hadn't been there the last time he had seen Tisdale. It was obvious that this case was personal, and the strain of disappointment and failure was getting to him.

'I propose that I continue following this man's trail,' Birch said. 'You go back to the Danes and give them a report on what we've learned so far.'

Tisdale looked away. 'We haven't learned much, except that Cannon's dead,' he replied with bitterness.

Birch was aware that this statement wasn't a reflection on his actions, but it stung nevertheless. If he hadn't been forced to kill Cannon to save Tisdale, they probably wouldn't have gotten much more out of the man anyway. Revenge was a strong motivation for maintaining silence. From the little time Birch had spent with Cannon, he had gotten the impression that the man didn't care about anyone else's anguish except his own— and that included a small, helpless girl.

'You're right,' Tisdale said into the silence. 'Someone's got to tell Hal and Marie that Cannon's dead. I'm the best one to break the news.'

'You can tell them that we've got another

lead and that I'm on the trail.'

Tisdale gave Birch a bleak look. 'Of course. I'll let them know.' He wheeled his horse around, then turned in his saddle. 'You'll wire us with any news?'

Birch nodded.

'Tell me honestly, Birch. With Cannon dead, do you think there's a chance we'll ever know what happened to Hannah?'

At that moment, looking Tisdale in the eye was the hardest thing Birch had ever done. 'Yes,' he replied, 'there's a chance.'

He saw determination and purpose return to Tisdale's face just before he rode away. Tisdale's back was even a little straighter.

CHAPTER EIGHTEEN

Birch followed the trail until he came to another small town, Cristo, its main street muddy from a recent spring rain. The man Birch was after had ridden down Cristo's main street, the impressions of his horse's recently shod hooves mingling with crisscrossed ruts of supply wagons and other hoofprints. Birch scanned the town, looking for any sign of the stranger, knowing that he had assigned himself an impossible task. If he had had any chance of apprehending this man, it would have happened before Cristo, Birch told himself.

Still, he knew he would go through the motions.

Birch started to dismount from Cactus at the first saloon on the main street, but an idea suddenly came to him. Osgood had mentioned that the stranger rode a pinto. Although pintos weren't rare, they were an unusual breed around this area. Pintos tended to be more common near the Mexican border. Birch directed Cactus down the middle of the main street, looking right and left. He spied a pinto tethered outside a small eating establishment. After leaving Cactus outside at the hitching post, he entered the restaurant.

The room was filled with workingmen eating their noon meal at long tables and benches. The special seemed to be some kind of stew— every customer in the place had a bowl in front of him.

Two harried young women bustled from kitchen to table, carrying steaming bowls of stew, plates of homemade bread, and tin pails of foamy beer. The kitchen was not separated by a wall but, rather, was located in the back of the large room. A muscular man, probably in his fifties, presided over a vat of stew. When he turned around, it was clear to Birch that this was a family business and that the two women who waited on the customers were the cook's daughters.

One of the young women stopped in front of Birch long enough to point out a free spot at the end of one of the tables. Birch complied, and a few minutes later found stew, bread, and beer placed in front of him. He paid the woman, then ate and drank in silence as he was forced to overhear a boisterous conversation between two men who were sharing his table.

'How's your girl, George?' one man asked between bites of bread.

'Growin' like a weed,' George replied when he had drained his beer. He reached over and poured more from the pail into his mug, liberally splashing the table surface as well. 'She's lookin' as pretty as her mama once did.'

'Boys'll be linin' up to court her in a few years,' his friend said.

'Prob'ly so. Guess I'll find out soon enough.'

'I know my boy's startin' to look her way.'

George looked at his friend sharply. The friend took note and raised his hands in self-defense. 'I've already talked to the boy, told him Ellen's too young. But I hope you won't mind if, in a few years, he comes courtin'.'

While Birch tried to ignore this conversation, he scanned the room, hoping to spot the man in the black and gray poncho. The air was muggy with the sweat of bodies crammed into the room, and Birch doubted very much that the man he was looking for would be wearing the poncho while he was eating.

Birch got up, taking his bowl and mug over to a table in the back where customers could leave their dirty dishes. The younger of the two women was stacking dirty plates. She was pretty in a wispy way, light brown hair caught up in back in a braid, large brown eyes, and a spray of freckles across her nose. One of the men passed by and caught her by the waist, pulling her close to him. He was small, but looked strong and wiry. He smelled heavily of beer. She struggled to get away, but he laughed and held her fast.

'Sir, let me go,' she ordered.

'Katy, I've seen you around here for the past few weeks, and I want to get to know you better,' the man said, swaying slightly. 'Maybe we can meet after your work is done here. I can show you a good time.'

The cook came over, brandishing a dripping stirring spoon. 'Let her go, damn it. That's my daughter, not some crib whore you can manhandle for a few pennies.'

The man grinned nastily and roughly pushed her away. 'Maybe you'd like a piece of me, old man.' The customer beckoned to the girl's father. 'Come on, you probably want to hit me. Go ahead.'

Birch had quietly sneaked up behind the man and now stuck his Navy Colt just behind his ear. 'I think you'd better leave,' he said softly. 'And I don't think your company is welcome here anymore.'

'That's right,' the father added gruffly. 'Don't come back or you're likely to go away with a big headache from the flat side of my skillet.'

The man sneered, his eyes half-closed, then slumped to the floor. A second man, his hat in his hand, approached them. 'I'm sorely sorry, ma'am,' he said, nodding to the young woman. 'He gets this way when he has too much to drink. Dan, he don't mean nothing by it. Tomorrow, he won't even remember he did this to you. He won't bother you again.'

'He'd better not,' the cook replied, crossing his arms, and ignoring the fact that he had a dripping spoon in one hand.

'I think you'd better get him out of here,' Birch suggested. The drunken man was starting to stir. Birch helped the second man pick his friend up off the floor and sling an arm around the sober man's neck.

'Thank you, sir,' the young woman said to Birch after the doors closed behind the two men. Her cheeks were flushed from the excitement.

'Your father seemed to have everything under control,' Birch allowed.

'Damn right,' the old man replied, then grinned. 'You made sure the odds were in my favor, though.'

Birch smiled back.

'Katy,' her father said, 'give this man his money back. His meal's on me.'

Katy began to dig into her apron pockets. Birch stopped her. 'I appreciate the thought,

123

but maybe you could repay me by answering a few questions instead.'

Katy's father nodded. 'Go ahead. We're happy to oblige.'

'Did a man wearing a black and gray poncho come in here?'

Katy frowned in concentration. 'I can't recall.' Her older sister walked by and she called to her. 'Delia, did a man in a black and gray poncho come in here earlier?'

Delia shook her head. 'I don't recollect.'

'He rides a pinto. It's tethered outside your restaurant right now.'

The two women and their father followed Birch to the window and looked out. The pinto was gone. Birch felt his shoulders slump. 'I'm sorry to have troubled you like this. I guess whoever owned the pinto wasn't the man I was looking for.'

As he turned to leave, a man approached. He had tousled black hair and wore faded denims. 'Excuse me, but I couldn't help overhearing. That man sat next to me, the one with the poncho. He left just a few minutes ago.'

Birch nodded his thanks.

'I was sitting facing the window,' the man went on to say, 'and I saw him head north up the main street.'

'Jim,' Katy said, clapping the customer on his shoulder, 'you just earned yourself a free beer.'

Birch thanked everyone once again and left.

124

He rode down the main street, keeping an eye out for the pinto. He came to the edge of town, slightly disappointed that the man on the pinto hadn't stopped at a general store or a saloon before heading out of town.

Birch headed back on the same road he had traveled with Tisdale. He thought briefly about his employer, hoping that Tisdale would go straight back to Deadwood and make his report to Hal Dane.

He traveled until it was dusk, then stopped in a flat area surrounded by boulders to make camp for the night. The next morning, he resumed his tracking. Considering that he had left the restaurant only minutes afterward, he began to wonder why he hadn't found the man in the poncho yet. Birch feared that he had missed something along the way. He was getting weary of tracking the elusive Hannah, but the guilt of killing the only connection to Hannah kept him riding.

A light spring rain began, a misting that had come over the distant mountains in a haze. The wildflowers along the road turned their thirsty petals up toward the sky to drink in the water. Birch stopped for a moment and pulled a canvas poncho out of his saddlebags. As he looked around to orient himself, he spied a building in the distance. He vaguely remembered passing it on the way to Redmesa.

It was little more than a glorified shack with an unusual number of hitching posts outside. If

Birch hadn't witnessed a man coming out the front door, pulling his braces up over his long johns, he would still have guessed that this was a brothel from the long line of tethered horses. And one of the horses was a pinto.

Birch dismounted and tethered Cactus next to the pinto. As he adjusted Cactus's saddle, he took a quick look at the pinto's saddle. The weather had warmed up enough that he had been certain the man he was tracking had taken off his poncho. Under the bedroll, Birch caught a glimpse of something gray and black, possibly a poncho. It was enough for him to want to find the pinto's owner.

The inside of the brothel had a packed dirt floor. Makeshift chairs and rickety old settees were scattered around the 'waiting area.' About ten men sat or milled around, smoking cheroots and hand-rolled cigarettes, slicking their hair down or combing their mustaches with their fingers, waiting for their turn. An open door on the far side of the room turned into a long, narrow hall with numerous doorways on either side, many of them having only a curtain to cover the entry.

Birch could hear a woman shrieking at a customer who had apparently already used her services and didn't have the money to pay. The customer burst through one of the curtained rooms, the prostitute right on his heels. He was tucking in his shirttails, a repentant look on his face. She wore a dingy corset and stained bloomers, but her feet and legs were bare.

'What do you think I run here, a charity?' the prostitute was asking him. 'You don't got the money, you don't get the service. You're ruining it for all my good customers, you come in here, use me, then don't pay.'

The customer turned around, gesturing in a placating manner. 'Rosie, put it on my tab. I promise I'll pay up the next time I come through here.' He headed toward the entrance.

Rosie threw her hands in the air. 'The next time he comes here, he says. And how many times is that, you might ask?' She was addressing the roomful of men. 'Two, maybe three times a year.' Rosie put a hand on her hip and looked around the room. 'Okay, who's next?' A timid-looking man, who was worrying the hat brim he held in his hands, stood up. Rosie nodded and gestured sharply toward the hall. 'Let's go.' As she ushered the man down the hall, Birch and the rest of the men could hear her saying, 'But I expect payment in advance, Jack.'

Birch met the eyes of a couple of the other potential customers, but most of them quickly averted their gazes. He studied each of them, trying to match the men with Osgood's description, but it was difficult for him to decide without the poncho. He stayed near the entrance, watching the men as they left. He had been there for what seemed like an hour, but what in reality was probably only ten minutes when a dirty-faced urchin came around the side of the building. No doubt it was the child of one of the prostitutes.

Birch felt a pang of sympathy for the child. It couldn't be an easy life, and certainly not a wholesome one for a child. Still, he could see that the child, a little girl, was carrying a rag doll. At least her mother had provided something for the little girl to occupy herself with, unlike so many children Birch had witnessed in similar circumstances.

Suddenly, Birch felt as if a bucket of cold water had been thrown at him. He bolted out the door, then stopped, remembering that he didn't want to try to talk to a squalling, frightened child. He slowed down and approached the little girl, who was fussing with the doll's yellow yarn hair.

She looked up when his shadow fell across her. Through the dirt, Birch could see that she was a delicate child, pretty, with plaited pale red hair and a scattering of freckles across her milky skin. She studied him. 'Hello.'

Birch crouched down to her level. 'Good day. That's a nice doll you have.'

'Her name is Irma. She's my new friend,' the girl said in a matter-of-fact tone. 'My name is Mary. What's yours?'

He told her.

Mary nodded solemnly. 'Mr Birch. Jefferson. Are you here to see my mama?'

'No. Actually, I wanted to know where you

got that doll. Irma.'

Mary suddenly paled and her eyes grew wide. She hugged the doll to herself. 'I've had her for a long time,' she said in a thin voice.

Birch smiled. 'She looks so new. How long is a long time?'

Mary squeezed her eyes shut and her grip on Irma relaxed. 'Are you going to take her away from me?'

Birch took a moment to answer. 'No, Mary. I won't take Irma away from you. I just want to know who gave you the doll.'

Mary opened her eyes and smiled. 'There he is. He gave me the doll. Told me to go outside and play while he talked to my mama.' She pointed to a man who was coming out of the brothel, a man who fit Osgood's description. Birch turned back to Mary, who was fussing with Irma again. In a singsong voice, she added, 'But I knew he didn't want to talk to my mama.'

'You're a smart little girl,' Birch replied. He took a coin out of his pocket and gave it to her. 'The next time your mama takes you into town, this is for some penny candy.'

She took it, her eyes almost as wide as the coin in her palm. Birch stood up and walked toward the man who was getting ready to ride.

'Excuse me,' Birch said. 'I need to ask you a question about that doll the little girl has.'

The man gave Birch a startled look, then dug

his spurs into his pinto and took off at a gallop, leaving Birch standing in the dust.

CHAPTER NINETEEN

Hal Dane put his pen down. He hadn't been able to work on his editorial since he'd come to the office a few hours before. He couldn't believe his luck—another lead to follow in the disappearance of his daughter. A woman had come to their door that morning. She said her name was Alice Cox, and that she had stayed the night in Deadwood. Miss Cox had read a copy of the *Deadwood Gazette* the night before and had been impressed by the striking resemblance between the etching of Hannah Dane and a young girl she had seen up in Silverton the week before.

If only Tisdale hadn't left a few days before, they could follow the clue now. He looked down at his editorial and realized that he had been staring at it for almost half an hour. He was too agitated to write. He got up and moved around, stretching his arms and rolling his shoulders in an effort to work out the kinks.

Maybe he should go to Silverton himself. He had promised Tisdale that he wouldn't interfere in their investigation, but then, this wasn't part of their investigation yet. The more he thought about the idea, the more he liked it. He didn't think he could sit back for the next few days, hoping Arthur would come back to town with news, and what harm would it do to go there?

He locked up the office and headed home to tell Marie of his decision.

'I'm not sure this is such a good idea,' his wife told him. She was working on a new doll, just like the one she had made for Hannah's birthday. It kept her busy and somehow made her feel close to Hannah.

'What do you mean? Don't you think I'm capable of following this lead?'

'Of course you are, Hal.' Marie's head was bent over her work. Dane could not see her expression, but he heard the fear in her voice. 'I'm just afraid of being left alone with the boys.'

'Oh, Marie, I won't let anything happen to you and the boys, I promise. I'm so sorry my involvement with the Anatoly case has put this family in jeopardy,' Dane said in a gentle voice, cupping her chin in his hand and tilting her head up until their eyes met.

Marie laid a cool hand on his hand. 'Don't blame yourself, Hal. You did what was right. The only one who is responsible for this is Stu Cannon.'

'We'll wait until tomorrow morning. If Arthur returns by then, we'll let him take care of it. Otherwise, I'll leave in the morning, and I promise I won't be gone long. Chances are that it's not Hannah. It should take me two days at most.'

She gave him a faint smile. 'Go ahead. We'll be all right.'

Dane started early the next morning, riding through an empty Deadwood, hoping to reach Silverton by noon. The morning air was cool, and the aspen groves along the trail were dotted with rabbitbrush and flowering serviceberry bushes.

Dane heard the pounding hooves coming up behind him and pulled his horse over to the side, assuming it was a rider who was in an awful hurry to get to the next town. Then he heard his name called out.

'Dane! Hal Dane!'

Dane peered around his shoulder, pulling up on the reins to stop his horse, but he couldn't see around the bushes that grew almost into the trail. Suddenly, Darnell Webb crashed through the brush and came to a sudden stop.

'Marshal, what are you doing here? Is there news of Hannah?' Dane leaned forward eagerly.

'As a matter of fact, there is,' Webb said.

'Has someone found her?' Dane asked, his voice full of desperation and hope.

Webb had a funny smile on his face, almost a nervous smile. 'No, Mr Dane. She hasn't been found, but I do have some news for you. A message from a friend of mine. Now why don't you get down from your horse there and we'll have a little discussion.'

'Marshal,' Dane said, trying to keep his impatience from showing, 'I'm afraid I don't have time for this. Maybe we can discuss it on the way to Silverton. Someone, a woman, thinks she spotted Hannah there.'

The marshal looked somber for a moment. 'This can't wait, Dane. I wouldn't worry too much about the sighting in Silverton. I set it up to get you out of Deadwood.'

It took a second for this information to sink in. Dane had enough control over himself to dismount from his horse. Webb followed suit.

'I don't understand, Marshal. What's this all about?'

'My friend knows where your daughter is.'

Dane ran toward him. 'Are you sure? Who is this friend? Where is he?' Dane strained his neck to look around the marshal, as if this friend was hiding behind him.

Webb took out Cannon's letter and handed it to Dane. Within seconds the newspaperman grimaced in horror at the contents of the letter.

'This is crazy! Marshal, you've got to do something...'

'Seems to me there's nothing anyone can do.'

Dane suddenly realized that Webb was protecting Cannon and had no intention of trying to find Hannah. He grabbed Webb and said, 'When did you get this letter? Where is Cannon now?'

The marshal shook him off as easily as if

133

Dane had been a bothersome child. 'If you ever lay a hand on me again, I'll kill you.'

But passion overtook good sense, as the grieving father saw Webb as his last link to his missing child.

'Damn you,' he said, throwing a wild punch that landed on the side of Webb's head. The marshal staggered briefly, but kept hold of his gun. Then he straightened up, a hard look on his face as he held his gun by the barrel and hit Dane with the butt. It took almost half a dozen blows to Dane's head before he blacked out.

CHAPTER TWENTY

Tisdale felt as if he were dragging a ten-ton wagon behind him as he guided his horse toward the Dane house, which loomed up ahead. He had stopped in Durango for the night, and had reached Deadwood in the early morning. Before going out to the house, Tisdale had stopped by Hal Dane's office, hoping to talk privately with his friend. But Hal wasn't there.

Tisdale didn't want to confront Marie just yet. He didn't think he could bear to look in her eyes when he gave her his report. When he had left Birch, there was a lead to follow, and Birch would follow it until he was satisfied, to the ends of the earth. But Tisdale didn't see much hope for finding his goddaughter.

It wasn't that Tisdale didn't have faith in Birch, it had just been so damn long since Hannah had disappeared, and he could almost see the chances of finding her dwindling with each new day. Birch was a damn fine tracker, but he wasn't a miracle worker.

The house looked empty. He figured the boys would be in school, but where were Marie and Hal? Tisdale dismounted and went up to the door. He could hear the clang of the metal knocker echoing through the hollow halls. Peering through a lace-curtained window to the right of the door, Tisdale could see that it was dark and closed up inside. He was about to leave when he decided to go around back. There was wash, still wet, hanging on the line. Tisdale called out, 'Marie? Hal?' He tried again. The third time he called, he caught a glimpse of white and blue in the woods, moving toward the house. Marie emerged from the young aspen trees on the edge of their property.

'Arthur!' Her eyes lit up. 'You got news for us?' She looked around. 'I notice that Mr Birch isn't with you.'

'Mr Birch is following another clue.'

The light in Marie's eyes died. 'Then you haven't been successful. I mean, you didn't find Stuart Cannon.'

Tisdale closed his eyes. 'We found him, Marie,' he said softly.

She leaned forward eagerly. 'You did?'

'He—he wouldn't tell us anything. He jumped me and was ready to kill me. Birch got to the scene in time to stop him.' He fell silent, hoping she would understand without having to hear the words.

She understood. 'He's dead?' Marie led him inside to the kitchen. 'Then the clue your agent is following is something Cannon said before he died.'

'Something like that. Actually, it's quite a good lead. It just seemed that it would be best if I came back here to report everything to you. Birch is best left to track alone.'

Marie turned toward Tisdale and forced a smile. 'I suppose you know best, Arthur.' She reached out and put a hand on his shoulder. 'I trust your judgment.'

She gestured for him to sit at the table. 'You must be hungry. Let me fix a meal for you.'

'Where's Hal?'

She busied herself with cutting homemade bread and cold meat. 'A woman came out to our house this morning with another lead. Hal has gone to follow it. I couldn't stop him.'

'Perhaps you'd better tell me where he's gone. If there's any trouble, Hal may need someone with him.'

Marie set the plate before him and gently pressed on his shoulder. 'Eat this while I tell you the details. You look as if you haven't eaten or slept properly for days.'

He ate while Marie told him that a woman who said she had come in on the stagecoach the night before had read Hal's plea in the latest *Gazette*. She remembered seeing a small girl like the one in the accompanying engraving— she thought it had been just a few days ago. It was on a farmhouse, she couldn't remember exactly where, but she thought it was on a road between Durango and Silverton. Marie went on to tell Tisdale that the woman had said her name was Alice Cox and that she would be staying in Deadwood at the Deadwood Hotel.

After Tisdale finished his meal, Marie saw him off at the front door. 'Tell my husband he'd better be home by tomorrow,' she called to him. 'The boys can't do the printing by themselves.'

Tisdale touched his hat and turned his horse in the direction of Silverton. When he reached Deadwood, Tisdale decided to call on Alice Cox at the Deadwood Hotel and question her a little further. It was very likely that Marie and Hal had gotten all the information Miss Cox was able to recall, but Tisdale always thought it best to double-check the source.

At the hotel desk, he asked the clerk for Miss Alice Cox's room number. The clerk glanced at the registration page and shook his head. 'I'm sorry, sir, there is no one by that name staying here.'

Tisdale frowned. Maybe Marie had gotten the name of the hotel wrong. Or maybe Miss

137

Cox hadn't found the accommodations suitable. He went on down the street, stopping at the other hotel and asking if Alice Cox was staying there. His query was met with a resounding no. Tisdale even tried the two boardinghouses, but no one had ever heard of a woman by that name.

Tisdale got back on his horse and began to head out of town toward Silverton. As he got to the edge of town, the marshal was riding into town. He glanced at Tisdale, scowled as if trying to place him, then rode on. Tisdale was tempted to go after the lawman and ask him if he knew anything about Alice Cox, but he recalled that Marshal Webb was a supporter of Stu Cannon and probably wouldn't be too sympathetic to Tisdale's dilemma. Tisdale rode on without slowing down.

Out on the road, the sun mercilessly beat down on his hat until he felt as if his head were in an oven. Tisdale finally took off his hat and wiped the sweat that had accumulated under his hatband. He had been traveling in the direction of Silverton for almost an hour when he saw a riderless horse up ahead. As he approached it, he realized that the animal looked an awful lot like one of Dane's horses. Tisdale slowed down and drew his Smith and Wesson, just in case ... He stepped into the brush that grew thick along the side of the Silverton trail. He could hear the rush of water nearby, a small stream that ran parallel to the

138

trail for a few hundred yards.

'Hal?' he called out before realizing that it was probably unwise to do so. He heard a moan beyond a large bush, and he crashed through to the other side to find his friend lying on the ground, his face severely beaten. Hal was cradling his ribs and one of his legs was at an odd angle.

'Who did this to you?' Tisdale asked as he holstered his gun and bent to inspect the damage. All of his cavalry training began to come back to him. He withdrew a pocketknife that he kept for paring apples. It wasn't much, but it was large enough for the job at hand— cutting some branches from one of the young aspens to make a travois. His friend was in no shape to mount his horse for the ride back to town.

Dane coughed, blood trickling from the corner of his mouth. 'It was Webb. He had a letter from Cannon admitting he took Hannah. He said she's still alive but that we'd never see her again.'

Tisdale winced. 'Why did he send the letter to Webb and why did Webb attack you?'

'I guess I'm the one who attacked him, although I'm not much of a fighter.' Dane tried to smile, but found it to be too painful. 'Webb sent a woman to our house to give us a story about seeing Hannah in Silverton. I can't believe I was so gullible. I was willing to drop everything and run off on the slightest bit of

139

evidence that someone had seen Hannah somewhere.'

Tisdale took a large white handkerchief out of his pocket and wet it in the stream, then began cleaning his friend's wounds as best he could. 'Anyone would have done the same thing, Hal. Hannah's your daughter. Of course you'd jump at every possible lead. I hadn't been in touch with you for several days, Birch has been tracking a lead, and—'

'What did you find?' Hal asked.

'I found Cannon and followed him from Redmesa to Flora Vista. I wired Birch before I left Redmesa.'

'Where is Cannon now? Was Hannah with him?' Dane asked eagerly.

Tisdale met Dane's eyes. 'Cannon's dead. Birch shot him. He had to. It was either me or him. Hannah wasn't with him, hadn't been for the last couple of days. Cannon wouldn't talk. He lived long enough to tell us he would never tell us.' Tisdale gathered the travois poles and laid them out to begin assembling the carrier. 'I'm sorry, Hal.'

'Sorry? At least the bastard is dead. I can die knowing he won't ever hurt anyone else's child.'

But Dane was not dying, at least not from his immediate wounds. Tisdale took Dane into Deadwood to the doctor's office.

CHAPTER TWENTY-ONE

Birch urged cactus on at a breakneck pace, determined not to let this man slip through his fingers like Cannon had done. After more than a mile, the man's horse began to tire and Cactus had the edge. When the horses were neck and neck, Birch maneuvered his horse close to the other horse, reached out, and grabbed a fistful of the man's shirt, yanking hard. The man gave a startled yell and pulled up on the reins of his horse. Cactus kept pace while Birch, with his other hand, drew his Colt and pressed it against the man's neck.

'Hold up,' he said.

The man put his hands in the air.

'No,' Birch said impatiently, 'stop your horse now. I just want to talk to you.'

The man blinked hard and tugged at the reins. Birch gestured for the man to dismount.

He was skinny to the point of emaciation, and he was trembling. 'You're not taking me in?' he stuttered.

Birch raised his eyebrows and waited. The man averted his eyes, his mustache twitching with anticipation. 'You're not the law?' he asked again.

'No. I wanted to ask you some questions about the man you met in Flora Vista, the one who gave you the package.'

141

The man flushed and stroked his mustache nervously. 'I don't know what you're talking about.'

'A brown paper package,' Birch explained patiently, his hand resting on the butt of his Colt. 'You met him across the street from a blacksmith's.'

The flush drained, and his eyes grew wide. He held his hands up in a gesture of surrender. 'All right, so I didn't deliver the package. But it was just a stupid rag doll. And that little girl back at that brothel never had a doll of her own.'

Birch lowered his gun slightly. 'I'd like to know about your meeting with the man who gave you the package.'

The man took a deep breath, then reached up and rubbed the back of his head. 'I stayed the night in Flora Vista. When I was getting ready to leave, a man came up to me. He was carrying a brown paper package. He asked me which way I was headed. When I told him north, he asked if I could deliver the package to a little girl. I was reluctant until he gave me a few dollars for my trouble.' He paused, avoiding Birch's steady gaze.

'Go on.'

The man cleared his throat and shifted nervously from one foot to the other. 'So I took the money and promised to deliver the package.' He chanced to look up at Birch, then quickly looked away. 'I got curious, what was

142

being sent. All sorts of things went through my mind—it was too light for gold, but it could be paper money, or bank drafts, or something I could sell.' He shook his head. 'When I finally opened it, I was disappointed to find a doll. Just a rag doll.'

'So you decided not to keep your word.'

The man stroked his mustache and frowned. 'It wasn't that. It was this little girl at the brothel. She just brightened when she saw it sticking out of my saddlebags. I couldn't take the doll away. I just couldn't.'

Birch holstered his gun. 'I understand. Now, can you tell me where you were supposed to deliver the package?'

The man blinked. 'Well, I was told to bear north and east for a day and a half. I'd come to a little farm with a corral on the south side of the house, a large cottonwood tree in front, and on the other side of the trail a field of paintbrush.'

'He didn't give you the name of a town near the farm, or the name of the people?' It was something, but it would be easier if he had a location to go on. Birch could stop by ten or a hundred farms before he found the right one.

The man had the grace to look sheepish. 'I forgot the name of the town, and he didn't give me the name of the people. He just told me that when I got there, it was easy to find and I'd know it when I saw it.'

Birch thanked the man. As he was about to

leave, he asked, 'When I caught up with you, you seemed to think I was the law. What are you running from?'

He grinned. 'I busted up a bar in Quicksilver, a town about two days' ride from here.'

Birch adjusted his hat. 'I doubt they'd be looking for you at this point. You're probably safe. I just wouldn't go back to Quicksilver anytime soon.'

The man touched his hat. 'Hope you find whatever it is you're searching for.'

'I hope so too.' Birch wheeled Cactus around and headed north and east across a grassy field that led to a series of low, rocky hills. It wasn't much to go on, but then when he'd started out, he'd had even less to go on and he'd gotten this far. Perhaps this would be the final piece of information that would lead him to Hannah Dane.

CHAPTER TWENTY-TWO

The next day, Birch kept heading north and east through one little town after another. He stopped in saloons and general stores to ask if a family in the area had just adopted a little girl. Each time he was met with rejection.

It was the afternoon of the second day when he rode into Howardsville, a little town in the valley between two low mountain ranges.

Cactus was limping; he'd lost a shoe earlier in the day and the going had been slow. Birch had walked Cactus the last few miles in the hot sun, and he was parched, ready for a beer and a meal.

Although Howardsville was small, the town looked prosperous. Smack in the middle of a large silver mining area, most of the people who lived there made their living from providing services and supplies to miners. Birch spied a blacksmith's shop and steered Cactus toward it.

A man sat on a bench outside the storefront, under the shade of a cottonwood tree. He studied Birch's approach. 'Your horse looks like he threw a shoe.'

'How soon can you fit him for another?' Birch asked.

The man got up and inspected Cactus's hooves. 'You might want a second one.' He held up one of the front hooves. 'This shoe's cracked.'

Birch nodded. 'Fine.'

'He'll be ready in a couple of hours.'

'Okay,' Birch replied. 'Is there a place nearby where I can get a meal?'

'Just down the road a piece.' The blacksmith pointed straight ahead.

'By the way, I'm looking for a family who might have adopted a little girl recently, just within the last week or so.'

The blacksmith nodded. 'Oh, yes. That

would be the Claymoores. They came to town the other day to introduce their new daughter, Anna. Right pretty little girl, about two or three. Shame her daddy left her.'

'Left her?'

The blacksmith nodded. 'He and the girl stayed on the Claymoore's property overnight. Mrs Claymoore, Helen is her name, she's a good woman. Feeds a lot of travelers looking for a meal and a place to sleep for a night. Anyway, when the Claymoores got up the next morning, the father was gone and the little girl was sitting in their yard, playing with the dog.' He looked up at Birch. 'Well, listen to me, talking your ear off. You probably want to get that meal.' Birch thanked him and walked over to an unnamed restaurant whose only advertisement was the savory smell wafting out of the open door. Inside, he sat down at a corner table and a woman came up to him.

'You look thirsty,' she said. She was a respectable-looking woman in her fifties. Her hair was salt-and-pepper, pulled back in a bun at the nape of her neck. Stray hairs clung to her forehead.

'I'd like a beer and a plate of whatever smells so good.'

She gave him a wide smile. 'Rabbit stew. I just made up a batch. I also just took a loaf of bread out of the oven.' She left, and five minutes later came back balancing a tray that contained a large bowl of stew, a loaf of bread,

146

a pail of beer, and an empty mug.

'You passing through?' she asked.

'My horse threw a shoe,' Birch explained. 'But I am looking for a couple, the Claymoores.'

'David and Helen Claymoore?'

'You know them?'

'Real nice people. Helen was just in town a while ago to buy some things for a little girl she took in. You know, they never had any children of their own. Little Anna was such a blessing, although I don't have much good to say about her father, leaving an innocent child like that with strangers. Thankfully, the Claymoores are an upstanding couple.'

Birch asked for directions to the Claymoore farm, and the woman was more than happy to give them in detail.

Two hours later, Birch was riding up to the Claymoore house, a modest wood dwelling with a swing on the porch and a large cottonwood tree out front. A field of red and orange paintbrush lay on the other side of the trail.

The young woman who came out on the porch as Birch dismounted must have seen him ride up.

'Can I help you?' she asked. She cocked her head in a friendly and open manner. Now that he knew their story, Birch was reluctant to be the bearer of bad news. If this was indeed Hannah, the Claymoores would probably be heartbroken. They might not be so quick to give her up, especially to a stranger. A small child came out and hung back by Helen Claymoore's skirts.

Birch took off his hat and crouched. 'Hannah?'

The solemn child pointed to herself. 'Anna!'

Mrs Claymoore's smile had turned to a concerned frown. 'Do you know this child?' Birch could see the glimmer of disappointment and heartbreak in her eyes.

'I think this child belongs to the people who hired me to find her.' Birch stood up and went over to Cactus. He reached into his saddlebags and took out the photograph of Hannah and the clipping of Hal Dane's editorial describing the abduction. He handed it to Mrs Claymoore. As she read it, the frown was replaced with genuine sorrow. A tear slid down her cheek.

'Helen?' The voice belonged to a tall dark-haired man who was probably in his late twenties. He had come from around the back of the house. 'Is something the matter? Is it bad news?' The man glanced at Birch, brushed past him, and was at his wife's side, one hand on Hannah's head.

'Oh, David, you have to read this,' Mrs Claymoore said as she handed the article and photograph to her husband. 'David, Anna didn't belong to the man who left her here. And we can't keep her.' The young woman folded

148

her arms protectively across her chest. 'We have to give her back.'

David Claymoore read the article silently, then stared at the photograph and the child by his side, comparing the two of them for a few long minutes. Hannah stared guilelessly up at him. 'Play?' she said before coming out from under her foster mother's skirts and down the stairs. She stopped in front of Birch and took his hand.

'Play?' she asked.

David Claymoore said, 'I think we'd better talk, Mr—?'

'Birch. Jefferson Birch.'

Helen Claymoore seemed to have pulled herself together. 'Would you like a glass of lemonade, Mr Birch?' She gestured toward the front door.

Birch took off his hat in deference to her. 'That would be fine.'

CHAPTER TWENTY-THREE

The doctor came out of his surgery with his sleeves rolled up. He was drying his hands on a clean white towel. 'Well, Mr Tisdale, Hal Dane has a good friend in you. I know the area where you found him, and if you hadn't come along, no one would have found him for days.'

'Then he'll be all right?' Tisdale asked.

'A few days in bed, and time to heal the bruises. His nose was broken, so he'll have a souvenir of his little run-in, but he should be fine.' The doctor paused, then asked, 'Hal wouldn't or couldn't tell me who did this to him. Tell me, was it road agents?'

Tisdale hesitated. He and Dane had agreed not to say anything about Webb for a while. If Birch's lead did not pan out, Webb might be their last hope of finding Hannah.

'I'm not sure,' Tisdale replied. 'But thank goodness, he's all right.'

*　　*　　*

The wire came to the Dane household the day after Hal Dane had been attacked. Tisdale had gone into town to check for messages. He rode back to the house in record time.

'Hal, Marie! Birch has found her,' he called out.

Marie practically flew down the stairs. Hal took longer, using the bannister to help him downstairs.

'Is she all right? Where is she? Is he sure it's Hannah?' The words tumbled past Marie's lips rapid-fire before Tisdale could answer her first question.

'Hannah is fine. She's safe,' he told both weary parents. Dane's legs wobbled underneath him and Tisdale helped him into a chair. The news had the opposite effect on Marie.

150

She seemed instantly energized, almost dancing around with joy and relief.

'Thank God she's okay,' Marie said, as tears ran down her cheeks. She bent over and hugged her husband. Then she stood and touched Tisdale's hand. 'And thank *you*, Arthur. Please—tell us when we can go get our baby.'

Tisdale read the wire aloud. 'Birch did not give a lot of details, but he said that Hannah was unharmed and he would be arriving with her tomorrow.'

When the boys got home from school, they were overjoyed to know that their sister would be coming home the next day. It was the first time since the day he had shown up that Tisdale had seen Conrad and Edgar so carefree.

'Does that mean we stay home from school?' Conrad asked shyly.

Hal laughed, a sound that Tisdale realized he hadn't heard in the Dane household since he had come to stay. 'I guess you can stay home and help your mother get things ready for your sister and Mr Birch.'

The rest of the day and that night seemed to go by slowly. Everyone was anxious for the next twenty-four hours to pass. Just before Tisdale was ready to turn in for the night, Hal limped into the study. 'Arthur? I need to talk to you for a moment.' He looked solemnly at his old friend. 'Do you think Hannah will be okay?

I'm worried that Cannon might have mistreated her.'

Tisdale wasn't sure what to say. He had not gotten the impression from his encounter with Cannon that he would have been rough with the child, but who knew where Cannon had left her or what might have happened to her before Birch found her. It was also possible that Hannah wouldn't remember anything about Cannon as time passed. She was two years old and Tisdale didn't know how much a child that age would remember.

'Hal, don't worry. Just be glad she's alive and safe. I don't know if she'll remember any of this, but Hannah will soon be back with her family, and with all the love and concern you have for your daughter, I'm sure she will heal quickly.'

The next day, the Danes were finishing breakfast at the table when Tisdale finally came downstairs. Marie was scrubbing down everything in the kitchen, the boys were talking in an animated manner, and even Hal was moving more easily than he had the day before. His bruises were fading, and he was using his bad arm again. He still wore a bandage around his head, but his eyes were twinkling and he smiled more. Even over the noisy babble of Conrad and Edgar, Tisdale could hear Marie humming cheerily.

A knock at the door sent everyone sprinting down the hall, with Hal Dane arriving last.

'They couldn't be here already,' Marie said as she smoothed back a stray wisp of hair and opened the door.

Birch stood there, hat in hand. Marie strained to look around his tall frame. 'They're coming, Mrs Dane,' he said. 'The Claymoores are coming by wagon and asked me to ride up ahead to let you know they'll be here with Hannah in about an hour.'

'Who are the Claymoores?' she asked.

'They are the family who has been looking after Hannah for the last few days. Nice people who treated her like she was their own.'

Marie's lips quivered as she worked at keeping her emotions under control.

'Birch!' Tisdale said as Marie made room for him to step out on the porch to greet his agent. 'You're sure the child you found is Hannah?'

Birch smiled. 'Oh, yes, I'm sure.' He dug into a pocket on the inside of the vest he wore, brought out the photograph, and handed it to Marie.

'I can't thank you enough, Mr Birch.' She turned to Tisdale and smiled affectionately. 'You, too, Arthur.' She reached out and squeezed his shoulder.

'Where is she? When's Hannah coming?' Conrad asked, as he and his brother stood in the doorway ahead of their father.

'She'll be along in a little while,' she told them. 'Let's go back inside and finish getting everything ready. Come on, boys.'

After Marie had gone inside, Dane limped out onto the porch. Tisdale related the events of the day before.

When he had finished, Birch rubbed his jaw. 'Now that Hannah's safe, I think I'll go into Deadwood and pay the marshal a little visit. Want to come along?'

Tisdale nodded silently, then went inside to get the gun he rarely wore.

Dane said to Birch, 'I can't tell you how much I'd like to go with you two.'

'We'll give Webb the message for you, don't worry.'

Tisdale added, 'We may not be back when the Claymoores arrive with Hannah, and I know you wouldn't want to miss seeing Hannah come home for the world.'

'You're right about that,' Dane said, settling into a chair by a window so he could keep watch for the Claymoores.

'What's our plan, Birch?' Tisdale asked as they rode toward Deadwood.

'I don't suppose anyone else saw the marshal show Dane the letter or pistol-whip him?'

'No, but the doctor can testify to Dane's injuries.'

'Maybe we should go to the mayor—he's the only one in town with the authority to take Webb's badge away.' Birch paused, then added, 'When we get to town, why don't you go find the mayor. I'll find Webb and keep an eye on him. He might run out if he finds out

Hannah is being returned to her family.'

Tisdale nodded in agreement. It didn't take long to find the mayor. After asking a few people, Tisdale was led right to him. He ran the biggest hotel in town.

'Sit down, Mr—I'm sorry, what was your name again?' Mayor Tom Potter was a tall, thin man with sunken cheeks, a thinning hairline, and circles under his eyes.

'Tisdale, sir. Arthur Tisdale.' He handed Potter one of his calling cards by way of introduction.

Mayor Potter examined it. 'So you're an investigator. Tell me what this is about.' He settled back in his chair to listen to what Tisdale had to tell him. When he was done, the mayor looked thoughtful.

'Well, I can't say I'm too surprised by this turn of events, Mr Tisdale. It was no secret that he sided with Stu Cannon during Hugh's trial. But I didn't think he'd have anything to do with kidnapping Dane's little girl. Even if he didn't know where Hannah was, he obstructed justice when he put Cannon's revenge over his duty.'

'My agent, Jefferson Birch, is looking for Webb right now, just to keep an eye on him and make sure he's not going to leave town before I talk to you.'

The mayor pushed himself out of his chair and grabbed his bowler hat. 'Let's go find Marshal Webb. Do you think your agent can

155

handle himself around a man like Webb?'

Tisdale nodded. 'I know so.'

'Webb spends most of his time at The Big D saloon. We'll look there first.'

When they got to The Big D, Birch wasn't anywhere to be seen. But Webb was inside, seated at a corner table with a glass and a whiskey bottle in front of him, his back to the wall. He didn't look so tough to Tisdale, and he started forward. The mayor held him back. 'Maybe we should wait outside for your agent.'

But Webb had already seen them. He gave them a nasty smile and said, 'Why don't you gentlemen join me?'

Tisdale looked around. No one was in The Big D except for the bartender, who was at the other end of the bar watering the whiskey bottles. The mayor sat and Tisdale followed.

'What brings you down here, Mayor? You never come into this saloon, if you can help it,' Webb said.

'We've come about Hal Dane,' Tisdale said.

'Oh, I heard what happened. It's all over town that someone beat him up pretty bad.' Webb poured himself a shot of whiskey and slugged it back. Then he grimaced and shook his head. 'Way I hear, it was road agents. Maybe I'd better ride out to Dane's and see if there's anything I can do.'

'You've done more than enough,' the mayor said in a tired voice. 'I'm here to relieve you of your badge.'

Webb looked around and laughed. 'I could take you and your friend easy.'

Tisdale knew that this was the bluster of a raving drunk. But Webb was the kind of man who was still dangerous even when he was drunk.

'Who's this man?' Webb asked, eyeing Tisdale for the first time.

'Hal Dane's friend, Arthur Tisdale,' a voice said from the other side of the saloon. Webb peered into the gloom. Tisdale strained his neck turning it around to see where Birch was, because he recognized his agent's voice.

'And who're you?' Webb said in a belligerent tone, as if Birch has spoiled his fun.

'Jefferson Birch. I'm here to make sure you hand your badge and your gun over to the good mayor there.'

Webb drew his pistol and pushed the muzzle into Mayor Potter's temple. 'And I've got my gun on the mayor here. So don't try anything.' Webb blinked, suddenly aware that Birch wasn't in sight anymore. 'Where are you, anyway? Come out where I can see you, dammit!'

There was a pause before Tisdale heard a floorboard creak. Webb jumped. The mayor's sweat pooled around the gun barrel.

'Webb, listen to me,' Tisdale said to distract him. 'Even if you killed the mayor and me, Birch will shoot you dead where you stand. Cannon's already dead. He tried to kill me, but

Birch killed him instead. Hannah's been safely returned to her family, so you see, it's all over. Don't make things worse for yourself.'

Webb looked sick at the realization that Cannon was dead. Suddenly he sneered. 'You're lying. I'd've been told if Cannon was dead.' Webb called out to the still invisible Birch. 'And if the girl had been found, I would've heard about it, too.'

'No one in town knows yet. Just give up before anyone else gets hurt.'

'Shut up! Let me think a minute.' There was almost resignation in his slurred words.

'Time's running out,' Tisdale said, trying to keep Webb off balance.

But his ploy backfired. Webb became enraged and turned his gun away from the mayor and toward Tisdale. He was about to pull the trigger when Birch bolted through the back door.

The crack of the shots came fast, so fast that Tisdale and the mayor barely had time to dive for cover behind a table. Seconds later, Birch was bent over, his smoking Colt in one hand, his other arm held tight to his body.

'Is it safe to come out?' the mayor murmured from behind Tisdale, who slowly looked around the side of the table. Webb lay in a pool of blood on the floor of The Big D.

Birch straightened up and holstered his gun. As Tisdale approached his agent, he noticed Birch's arm was bleeding.

Birch looked at Tisdale. 'He got me, but I think I'll live.'

'Good thing,' Tisdale replied with a crooked grin. 'I wouldn't know what to do with your pay if you hadn't made it.'

After Webb's body had been removed from the saloon, the mayor insisted on accompanying Birch and Tisdale out to the Danes' house. Hal and Marie Dane were still waiting for the Claymoores and Hannah.

'Are you sure they know how to get here?' Marie asked Birch.

He smiled. 'They'll be here. Travel is a bit slower by wagon. They should be here sometime soon.'

Tisdale and the mayor were telling Dane about Marshal Webb's last stand. 'Hal, Marie,' Mayor Potter said when the story was finally told, 'I just wanted you to know that I'm sorry for all the heartache you've had to go through these last few weeks.'

Marie invited the mayor in for a cup of coffee and a late breakfast, which he politely declined before departing.

CHAPTER TWENTY-FOUR

It was early afternoon when the wagon arrived with Hannah seated between a young couple. Marie tore the door open, calling to Hal and the boys. She picked up her skirts and ran with abandon, getting to the wagon just as the driver was helping Hannah down to the ground. 'Hannah!' She held her at arms' length for a moment, long enough for Hal to get to her side. Then the Danes hugged their daughter.

'Mommy, Daddy,' Hannah said. A moment later, she asked, 'Anna?'

Marie pulled away, understanding her daughter immediately. She shot a grateful look at the young couple and turned to Edgar, whispering something to him. He turned and ran back to the house.

Tisdale came over to Birch, who was pulling the saddle off Cactus. 'I don't know how you did it, Birch. There wasn't much to go on.'

Birch shrugged and almost smiled. 'I just got lucky.'

The two men looked over at the Danes, who were talking to the young couple. 'Helen and David Claymoore,' Birch said. 'They live in a little town about a day's ride from here, Howardsville. Cannon abandoned the child at their home.'

Tisdale nodded. Edgar came out of the house, carrying the new rag doll. Hannah ran toward him, her arms outstretched. 'New Anna!' Her smiling parents turned to watch her.

Helen Claymoore's voice drifted down to where Birch and Tisdale stood. 'So that's who Anna is. We'd been calling her Anna because

160

that's what she said when we asked her name.'

Marie Dane threaded her arm through Helen's and they walked toward Tisdale and Birch, relating the saga of Anna the rag doll.

When they reached the two men, Marie turned to Birch first. 'Thank you. I wish there was a better way of showing you how grateful I am, we are, than to just say those words.'

Birch touched the brim of his hat. 'Mrs Dane, watching Hannah is a reward in itself. I'm just thankful she wasn't hurt, or worse. And that I found her at all is a miracle in itself.'

Marie shook his hand. Hal was by her side and took the opportunity to shake Birch's hand while Marie turned to Tisdale. 'Arthur,' she said, a tear sliding down her face. 'You are such a good friend. But you're more than that, you're part of our family.' She embraced him and kissed his cheek. 'Thank you. I hope you plan to stay for a while, now that our family is whole again.'

'I'll stay for a few days,' he said. 'It's time I got to know my goddaughter and spent some time with the boys, now that almost everything's back to normal.'

It had been an emotional day for everyone. Marie took charge, bringing Helen inside to the parlor for tea. Hal supervised the setting up of a game of horseshoes. While Tisdale was checking the distance between the two poles, he noticed that Birch had saddled up Cactus again.

161

'Birch!' His agent turned around as Tisdale trotted over. 'You're not leaving, are you?'

Birch pushed his hat back. 'Well, the way I figure it, there's enough people here to keep Marie Dane hopping. I think this is the right time for me to go.'

'You're not an imposition,' Marie said in a strong, clear voice. She was standing behind them. 'I saw you getting ready to leave from my kitchen window, Jefferson Birch, and if you don't stay until that wound heals some, we will all be very upset.'

Hannah clung to her mother's skirt, her rag doll clutched in one hand. 'Stay.'

Tisdale turned to watch Birch's reaction. He knew Birch to be a loner, someone who liked to get back on the road the minute a job was finished. Hannah broke away from her mother and approached Birch, extending her new rag doll to him. 'Stay.'

Birch crouched, took the rag doll from Hannah, and looked at it. He looked up at Marie Dane's smiling face and stood up again. 'I guess I could stay the night.' He handed the rag doll back to Hannah and took Cactus's reins to lead him back to the corral.

Tisdale suppressed a smile.

We hope you have enjoyed this Large Print book. Other Chivers Press or G. K. Hall Large Print books are available at your library or directly from the publishers. For more information about current and forthcoming titles, please call or write, without obligation, to:

Chivers Press Limited
Windsor Bridge Road
Bath BA2 3AX
England
Tel. (01225) 335336

OR

G. K. Hall
P.O. Box 159
Thorndike, Maine 04986
USA
Tel. (800) 223–6121 (U.S. & Canada)
In Maine call collect: (207) 948–2962

All our Large Print titles are designed for easy reading, and all our books are made to last.